Published by POCKET BOOKS/WASHINGTON SQUARE PRESS

Agatha Christie
At Bertram's Hotel

PUBLISHED BY POCKET BOOKS NEW YORK

POCKET BOOKS, a division of Simon & Schuster, Inc.
1230 Avenue of the Americas, New York, N.Y. 10020

ISBN: 0-671-49452-4

First Pocket Books printing December, 1967

25 24 23 22 21 20 19 18 17

FOR HARRY SMITH
because I appreciate the scientific
way he reads my books

Cast of Characters

COLONEL DEREK LUSCOMBE—A good-natured, elderly widower, his old-fashioned ideas about women made him the inevitable pigeon.

LADY SELINA HAZY—An aging gentlewoman, her memory was sharper than her eyesight.

MISS GORRINGE—The perfect receptionist, she had an imperturbable manner that never changed, even when the walls came tumbling down.

HUMFRIES—A perfect manager of the most respectable hotel, he supplied his customers with whatever they wanted—no matter what the risk.

MISS JANE MARPLE—A lady who scented evil, suspected evil, and saw evil wherever she looked—she couldn't be sidetracked by a colossal fraud.

BESS SEDGWICK—One of the wild ones, she took her excitement where she found it.

ELVIRA BLAKE—Bess's daughter, she had the veneer of a finishing-school education, and the venery instincts of a tigress.

LADISLAUS MALINOWSKI—Racing-car driver, soldier of fortune, and Don Juan, he was bound to tangle with the wrong woman once too often.

7

CANON PENNYFATHER—The absentminded scholar, he went to the right place at the wrong time, and almost didn't live to regret it.

CHIEF INSPECTOR FRED DAVY—He had a fatherly image and an instinct for spotting the bad sprouts among the blossoms.

MICHAEL GORMAN—A simple man, he married for fun and discovered that the name of the game was murder.

BRIDGET—Despite her mother, she managed to be where things were happening—and even helped to make them happen.

MR. ROBINSON—Neither the name nor anything else about him was real—except the information he could give if he chose.

ROBERT HOFFMAN—A man so rich he considered a million-dollar robbery only a trivial incident.

1

In the heart of the West End, there are many quiet pockets, unknown to almost all but taxi drivers who traverse them with expert knowledge, and arrive triumphantly thereby at Park Lane, Berkeley Square, or South Audley Street.

If you turn off on an unpretentious street from the Park, and turn left and right once or twice, you will find yourself in a quiet street with Bertram's Hotel on the right-hand side. Bertram's Hotel has been there a long time. During the war, houses were demolished on the right of it, and a little farther down on the left of it, but Bertram's itself remained unscathed. Naturally it could not escape being, as house agents would say, scratched, bruised, and marked, but by the expenditure of only a reasonable amount of money it was restored to its original condition. By 1955 it looked precisely as it had looked in 1939—dignified, unostentatious, and quietly expensive.

Such was Bertram's, patronized over a long stretch of years by the higher echelons of the clergy, dowager ladies of the aristocracy up from the country, girls on their way home for the holidays from expensive finishing schools. ("So few places where a girl can stay alone in London but of course it is *quite* all right at Bertram's. We have stayed there for *years*.")

There had, of course, been many other hotels on the model of Bertram's. Some still existed, but nearly all had felt the wind of change. They had had necessarily to modernize themselves, to cater for a different clientele. Bertram's, too, had had to change, but it had been done so cleverly that it was not at all apparent at the first casual glance.

Outside the steps that led up to the big swing doors stood what at first sight appeared to be no less than a field marshal. Gold braid and medal ribbons adorned a broad and manly chest. His deportment was perfect. He received you with tender concern as you emerged with rheumatic difficulty from a taxi or a car, guided you carefully up the steps and piloted you through the silently swinging doorway.

Inside, if this was the first time you had visited Bertram's, you felt, almost with alarm, that you had re-entered a vanished world. Time had gone back. You were in Edwardian England once more.

There was, of course, central heating, but it was not apparent. As there had always been, in the big central lounge, there were two magnificent coal fires; beside them big brass coal scuttles shone in the way they used to shine when Edwardian housemaids polished them, and they were filled with exactly the right-sized lumps of coal. There was a general appearance of rich red velvet and plushy coziness. The armchairs were not of this time and age. They were well above the level of the floor, so that rheumatic old ladies had not to struggle in an undignified manner in order to get to their feet. The seats of the chairs did not, as in so many modern high-priced armchairs, stop halfway between the thigh and the knee, thereby inflicting agony on those suffering from arthritis and sciatica; and they were not all of a pattern. There were straight backs and reclining backs, different widths to accommodate the slender and the obese. People of almost any dimension could find a comfortable chair at Bertram's.

Since it was now the tea hour, the lounge hall was full. Not that the lounge hall was the only place where you could have tea. There was a drawing room (chintzy), a smoking room (by some hidden influence reserved for gentlemen only) where the vast chairs were of fine leather, two writing rooms, where you could take a special friend and have a cozy little gossip in a quiet corner—and even write a letter as well if you wanted to. Besides these amenities of the Edwardian age, there were other retreats, not in any way publicized, but known to those who wanted them. There was a double bar, with two bar attendants, an American barman to make the Americans feel at home and to provide them with bourbon, rye, and every kind of cocktail, and an English one to deal with sherries and Pimm's No. 1, and to talk knowledgeably about the runners at Ascot and Newbury to the middle-aged men who stayed at Bertram's for the more serious race meetings. There was also, tucked down a passage, in a secretive way, a television room for those who asked for it.

But the big entrance lounge was the favourite place for the afternoon tea drinking. The elderly ladies enjoyed seeing who came in and out, recognizing old friends, and commenting unfavourably on how these had aged. There were also American visitors fascinated by seeing the titled English really getting down to their traditional afternoon tea. For afternoon tea was quite a feature of Bertram's.

It was nothing less than splendid. Presiding over the

ritual was Henry, a large and magnificent figure, a ripe fifty, avuncular, sympathetic, and with the courtly manners of that long vanished species: the perfect butler. Slim youths performed the actual work under Henry's austere direction. There were large crested silver trays, and Georgian silver teapots. The china, if not actually Rockingham and Davenport, looked it. The Blind Earl services were particular favourites. The tea was the best Indian, Ceylon, Darjeeling, Lapsang, etc. As for eatables, you could ask for anything you liked—and get it!

On this particular day, November the 17th, Lady Selina Hazy, sixty-five, up from Leicestershire, was eating delicious well-buttered muffins with all an elderly lady's relish.

Her absorption with muffins, however, was not so great that she failed to look up sharply every time the inner pair of swing doors opened to admit a newcomer.

So it was that she smiled and nodded to welcome Colonel Luscombe—erect, soldierly, race glasses hanging round his neck. Like the old autocrat that she was, she beckoned imperiously and in a minute or two, Luscombe came over to her.

"Hello, Selina, what brings you up to Town?"

"Dentist," said Lady Selina, rather indistinctly, owing to muffin. "And I thought as I was up, I might as well go and see that man in Harley Street about my arthritis. You know who I mean."

Although Harley Street contained several hundreds of fashionable practitioners for all and every ailment, Luscombe did know whom she meant.

"Do you any good?" he asked.

"I rather think he did," said Lady Selina grudgingly. "Extraordinary fellow. Took me by the neck when I

12

wasn't expecting it, and wrung it like a chicken." She moved her neck gingerly.

"Hurt you?"

"It must have done, twisting it like that, but really I hadn't time to know." She continued to move her neck gingerly. "Feels all right. Can look over my right shoulder for the first time in years."

She put this to a practical test and exclaimed.

"Why I do believe that's old Jane Marple. Thought she was dead years ago. Looks a hundred."

Colonel Luscombe threw a glance in the direction of Jane Marple thus resurrected but without much interest; Bertram's always had a sprinkling of what he called fluffy old pussies.

Lady Selina was continuing.

"Only place in London you can still get muffins. Real muffins. Do you know when I went to America last year they had something called muffins on the breakfast menu. Not real muffins at all. Kind of teacake with raisins in them. I mean, why call them muffins?"

She pushed in the last buttery morsel and looked round vaguely. Henry materialized immediately. Not quickly or hurriedly. It seemed that, just suddenly, he was there.

"Anything further I can get you, my lady? Cake of any kind?"

"Cake?" Lady Selina thought about it, was doubtful.

"We are serving very good seed cake, my lady. I can recommend it."

"Seed cake? I haven't eaten seed cake for years. It is *real* seed cake?"

"Oh yes, my lady. The cook has had the receipt for years. You'll enjoy it, I'm sure."

Henry gave a glance at one of his retinue, and the lad departed in search of seed cake.

"I suppose you've been at Newbury, Derek?"

"Yes. Darned cold. I didn't wait for the last two races. Disastrous day. That filly of Harry's was no good at all."

"Didn't think she would be. What about Swanhilda?"

"Finished fourth." Luscombe rose. "Got to see about my room."

He walked across the lounge to the reception desk. As he went he noted the tables and their occupants. Astonishing number of people having tea here. Quite like old days. Tea as a meal had rather gone out of fashion since the war. But evidently not at Bertram's. Who *were* all these people? Two canons and the Dean of Chislehampton. Yes, and another pair of gaitered legs over in the corner, a Bishop, no less! Mere Vicars were scarce. Have to be at least a canon to afford Bertram's, he thought. The rank and file of the clergy certainly couldn't, poor devils. As far as that went, he wondered how on earth people like old Selina Hazy could. She'd only got twopence or so a year to bless herself with. And there was old Lady Berry, and Mrs. Posselthwaite from Somerset, and Sybil Kerr—all poor as church mice.

Still thinking about this he arrived at the desk and was pleasantly greeted by Miss Gorringe, the receptionist. Miss Gorringe was an old friend. She knew every one of the clientele and, like royalty, never forgot a face. She looked frumpy but respectable. Frizzled yellowish hair (old-fashioned tongs, it suggested), black silk dress, a high bosom on which reposed a large gold locket and a cameo brooch.

"Number fourteen," said Miss Gorringe. "I think you

had fourteen last time, Colonel Luscombe, and liked it. It's quiet."

"How you always manage to remember these things, I can't imagine, Miss Gorringe."

"We like to make our old friends comfortable."

"Takes me back a long way, coming in here. Nothing seems to have changed."

He broke off as Mr. Humfries came out from an inner sanctum to greet him.

Mr. Humfries was often taken by the uninitiated to be Mr. Bertram in person. Who the actual Mr. Bertram was, or indeed, if there ever had been a Mr. Bertram, was now lost in the mists of antiquity. Bertram's had existed since about 1840, but nobody had taken any interest in tracing its past history. It was just there, solid, a fact. When addressed as Mr. Bertram, Mr. Humfries never corrected the impression. If they wanted him to be Mr. Bertram, he would be Mr. Bertram. Colonel Luscombe knew his name, though he didn't know if Humfries was the manager or the owner. He rather fancied the latter.

Mr. Humfries was a man of about fifty. He had very good manners, and the presence of a junior minister. He could, at any moment, be all things to all people. He could talk racing shop, cricket, foreign politics, tell anecdotes of royalty, give motor show information, knew the most interesting plays on at present, advise on places Americans ought really to see in England however short their stay. He had knowledgeable information about where it would suit persons of all incomes and tastes to dine. With all this, he did not make himself too cheap. He was not on tap all the time. Miss Gorringe had all the same facts at her fingertips and could retail them efficiently. At brief intervals Mr. Humfries, like the sun, made his appearance above the horizon and flattered someone by his personal attention.

This time it was Colonel Luscombe who was so honoured. They exchanged a few racing platitudes, but Colonel Luscombe was absorbed by his problem. And here was the man who could give him the answer.

"Tell me, Humfries, how do all these old dears manage to come and stay here?"

"Oh you've been wondering about that?" Mr. Humfries seemed amused. "Well, the answer's simple. They couldn't afford it. Unless—"

He paused.

"Unless you make special prices for them? Is that it?"

"More or less. They don't really know, usually, that they are special prices, or if they do realize it, they think it's because they're old customers."

"And it isn't just that?"

"Well, Colonel Luscombe, I am running a hotel. I couldn't afford actually to lose money."

"But how can that pay you?"

"It's a question of atmosphere . . . Strangers coming to this country—Americans, in particular, because they are the ones who have the money—have their own rather queer ideas of what England is like. I'm not talking, you understand, of the rich business tycoons who are always crossing the Atlantic. They usually go to the Savoy or the Dorchester. They want modern décor, American food, all the things that will make them feel at home. But there are a lot of people who come abroad at rare intervals and who expect this country to be—well, I won't go back as far as Dickens, but they've read *Cranford* and Henry James, and they don't want to find this country just the same as their own! So they go back home afterwards and say:

'There's a wonderful place in London; Bertram's Hotel, it's called. It's just like stepping back a hundred years. It just is old England! And the people who stay there! People you'd never come across anywhere else. Wonderful old duchesses. They serve all the old English dishes, there's a marvellous old-fashioned beefsteak pudding! You've never tasted anything like it; and great sirloins of beef and saddles of mutton, and an old-fashioned English tea and a wonderful English breakfast. And of course all the usual things as well. And it's wonderfully comfortable. And warm. Great log fires.' "

Mr. Humfries ceased his impersonation and permitted himself something nearly approaching a grin.

"I see," said Luscombe thoughtfully. "These people; decayed aristocrats, impoverished members of the old country families, they are all so much *mise en scène*?"

Mr. Humfries nodded agreement.

"I really wonder no one else has thought of it. Of course I found Bertarm's ready made, so to speak. All it needed was some rather expensive restoration. All the people who come here think it's something that they've discovered for themselves, that no one else knows about."

"I suppose," said Luscombe, "that the restoration was quite expensive?"

"Oh yes. The place has got to look Edwardian, but it's got to have the modern comforts that we take for granted in these days. Our old dears—if you will forgive me referring to them as that—have got to feel that nothing has changed since the turn of the century, and our travelling clients have got to feel they can have period surroundings, and still have what they are used to having at home, and can't really live without!"

"Bit difficult sometimes?" suggested Luscombe.

"Not really. Take central heating for instance. Americans require—need, I should say—at least ten degrees Fahrenheit higher than English people do. We actually have two quite different sets of bedrooms. The English we put in one lot, the Americans in the other. The rooms all look alike, but they are full of actual differences—electric razors, and showers as well as tubs in some of the bathrooms, and if you want an American breakfast, it's there—cereals and iced orange juice and all—or if you prefer you can have the English breakfast."

"Eggs and bacon?"

"As you say—but a good deal more than that if you want it. Kippers, kidneys and bacon, cold grouse, York ham. Oxford marmalade."

"I must remember all that tomorrow morning. Don't get that sort of thing any more at home."

Humfries smiled. "Most gentlemen only ask for eggs and bacon. They've—well, they've got out of the way of thinking about the things there used to be."

"Yes, yes . . . I remember when I was a child. . . . Sideboards groaning with hot dishes. Yes, it was a luxurious way of life."

"We endeavour to give people anything they ask for."

"Including seed cake and muffins—yes, I see. To each according to his need—I see. . . . Quite Marxian."

"I beg your pardon?"

"Just a thought, Humfries. Extremes meet."

Colonel Luscombe turned away, taking the key Miss Gorringe offered him. A page boy sprang to attention and conducted him to the elevator. He saw in passing that Lady Selina Hazy was now sitting with her friend Jane Something or other.

2

"And I suppose you're still living at that dear St. Mary Mead?" Lady Selina was asking. "Such a sweet unspoiled village. I often think about it. Just the same as ever, I suppose?"

"Well, not quite." Miss Marple reflected on certain aspects of her place of residence. The new housing developments. The additions to the Village Hall, the altered appearance of the High Street with its up-to-date shop fronts. . . . She sighed. "One has to accept change, I suppose."

"Progress," said Lady Selina vaguely. "Though it often seems to me that it isn't progress. All these smart plumbing fixtures they have nowadays. Every shade of colour and superb what they call 'finish'—but do any of them really pull? Or push, when they're that kind. Every time you go to a friend's house, you find some kind of a notice in the Loo—'Press sharply and release,' 'Pull to the left,' 'Release quickly.' But in the old days, one just pulled up a handle any kind of way, and cataracts of water came at once—There's the dear Bishop of Medmenham," Lady Selina broke off to say, as a handsome, elderly cleric passed by. "Practically quite blind, I believe. But such a splendid militant priest."

19

A little clerical talk was indulged in, interspersed by Lady Selina's recognition of various friends and acquaintances, many of whom were not the people she thought they were. She and Miss Marple talked a little of "old days," though Miss Marple's upbringing, of course, had been quite different from Lady Selina's, and their reminiscences were mainly confined to the few years when Lady Selina, a recent widow of severely straitened means, had taken a small house in the village of St. Mary Mead during the time her second son had been stationed at an airfield nearby.

"Do you always stay here when you come up, Jane? Odd I haven't seen you here before."

"Oh no, indeed. I couldn't afford to, and anyway, I hardly ever leave home these days. No, it was a very kind niece of mine who thought it would be a treat for me to have a short visit to London. Joan is a very kind girl—at least perhaps hardly a girl." Miss Marple reflected with a qualm that Joan must now be close on fifty. "She is a painter, you know. Quite a well-known painter. Joan West. She had an exhibition not long ago."

Lady Selina had little interest in painters, or indeed in anything artistic. She regarded writers, artists, and musicians as a species of clever performing animals; she was prepared to feel indulgent towards them, but to wonder privately why they wanted to do what they did.

"This modern stuff, I suppose," she said, her eyes wandering. "There's Cicely Longhurst—dyed her hair again, I see."

"I'm afraid dear Joan is rather modern."

Here Miss Marple was quite wrong. Joan West had been modern about twenty years ago, but was now regarded by the young *arriviste* artists as completely old-fashioned.

Casting a brief glance at Cicely Longhurst's hair, Miss Marple relapsed into a pleasant remembrance of how kind Joan had been. Joan had actually said to her husband, "I wish we could do something for poor old Aunt Jane. She never gets away from home. Do you think she'd like to go to Bournemouth for a week or two."

"Good idea," said Raymond West. His last book was doing very well indeed, and he felt in a generous mood.

"She enjoyed her trip to the West Indies, I think, though it was a pity she had to get mixed up in a murder case. Quite the wrong thing at her age."

"That sort of thing seems to happen to her."

Raymond was very fond of his old aunt and was constantly devising treats for her, and sending her books that he thought might interest her. He was suprised when she often politely declined the treats, and though she always said the books were "so interesting," he sometimes suspected that she had not read them. But then, of course, her eyes were failing.

In this last he was wrong. Miss Marple had remarkable eyesight for her age, and was at this moment taking in everything that was going on round her with keen interest and pleasure.

To Joan's proffer of a week or two at one of Bournemouth's best hotels, she had hesitated, murmured, "It's very, very kind of you, my dear, but I really don't think—"

"But it's good for you, Aunt Jane. Good to get away from home sometimes. It gives you new ideas, and new things to think about."

"Oh yes, you are quite right there, and I would

like a little visit somewhere for a change. Not, perhaps, Bournemouth."

Joan was slightly surprised. She had thought Bournemouth would have been Aunt Jane's Mecca.

"Eastbourne? Or Torquay?"

"What I would really like—" Miss Marple hesitated.

"Yes?"

"I dare say you will think it rather silly of me."

"No, I'm sure I shan't." (Where did the old dear want to go?)

"I would really like to go to Bertram's Hotel—in London."

"Bertram's Hotel?" The name was vaguely familiar.

Words came from Miss Marple in a rush. "I stayed there once—when I was fourteen. With my uncle and aunt. Uncle Thomas, that was, he was Canon of Ely. And I've never forgotten it. If I could stay there—a week would be quite enough—two weeks might be too expensive."

"Oh, that's all right. Of course you shall go. I ought to have thought that you might want to go to London—the shops and everything. We'll fix it up—if Bertram's Hotel still exists. So many hotels have vanished, sometimes bombed in the war and sometimes just given up."

"No, I happen to know Bertram's Hotel is still going. I had a letter from there—from my American friend Amy McAllister of Boston. She and her husband were staying there."

"Good, then I'll go ahead and fix it up." She added gently, "I'm afraid you may find it's changed a good deal from the days when you knew it. So don't be disappointed."

But Bertram's Hotel had not changed. It was just

as it had always been. Quite miraculously so, in Miss Marple's opinion. In fact, she wondered. . . .

It really seemed too good to be true. She knew quite well, with her usual clear-eyed common sense, that what she wanted was simply to refurbish her memories of the past in their old original colours. Much of her life had, perforce, to be spent recalling past pleasures. If you could find someone to remember them with, that was indeed happiness. Nowadays that was not easy to do; she had outlived most of her contemporaries. But she still sat and remembered. In a queer way, it made her come to life again—Jane Marple, that pink and white eager young girl. . . . Such a silly girl in many ways . . . now who was that very unsuitable young man whose name—oh dear, she couldn't even remember it now! How wise her mother had been to nip that friendship so firmly in the bud. She had come across him years later—and really he was quite dreadful! At the time she had cried herself to sleep for at least a week!

Nowadays, of course—she considered nowadays. . . . These poor young things. Some of them had mothers, but never mothers who seemed to be any good—mothers who were quite incapable of protecting their daughters from silly affairs, illegitimate babies, and early and unfortunate marriages. It was all very sad.

Her friend's voice interrupted these meditations.

"Well, I never. Is it—yes, it is—Bess Sedgwick over there! Of all the unlikely places—"

Miss Marple had been listening with only half an ear to Lady Selina's comments on her surroundings. She and Miss Marple moved in entirely different circles, so that Miss Marple had been unable to exchange scandalous tidbits about the various friends or acquaintances that Lady Selina recognized or thought she recognized.

But Bess Sedgwick was different. Bess Sedgwick was a name that almost everyone in England knew. For over thirty years now, Bess Sedgwick had been reported by the press as doing this or that outrageous or extraordinary thing. For a good part of the war she had been a member of the French Resistance, and was said to have six notches on her gun representing dead Germans. She had flown solo across the Atlantic years ago, had ridden on horseback across Europe and fetched up at Lake Van. She had driven racing cars, had once saved two children from a burning house, had several marriages to her credit and discredit and was said to be the second best-dressed woman in Europe. It was also said that she had successfully smuggled herself aboard a nuclear submarine on its test voyage.

It was therefore with the most intense interest that Miss Marple sat up and indulged in a frankly avid stare.

Whatever she had expected of Bertram's Hotel, it was not to find Bess Sedgwick there. An expensive night club, or a lorry drivers' lunch counter—either of those would be quite in keeping with Bess Sedgwick's wide range of interests. But this highly respectable and old world hostelry seemed strangely alien.

Still there she was—no doubt of it. Hardly a month passed without Bess Sedgwick's face appearing in the fashion magazines or the popular press. Here she was in the flesh, smoking a cigarette in a quick impatient manner and looking in a surprised way at the large tea tray in front of her as though she had never seen one before. She had ordered—Miss Marple screwed up her eyes and peered—it was rather far away—yes, doughnuts. Very interesting.

As she watched, Bess Sedgwick stubbed out her cigarette in her saucer, lifted a doughnut and took an immense bite. Rich red real strawberry jam gushed out over her chin. Bess threw back her head and laughed, one of the loudest and gayest sounds to have been heard in the lounge of Bertram's Hotel for some time.

Henry was immediately beside her, a small delicate napkin proffered. She took it, scrubbed her chin with the vigour of a schoolboy, exclaiming: "That's what I call a real doughnut. Gorgeous."

She dropped the nakin on the tray and stood up. As usual every eye was on her. She was used to that. Perhaps she liked it, perhaps she no longer noticed it. She was worth looking at—a striking woman rather than a beautiful one. The palest of platinum hair fell sleek and smooth to her shoulders. The bones of her head and face were exquisite. Her nose was faintly aquiline, her eyes deep set and a real grey in colour. She had the wide mouth of a natural comedian. Her dress was of such simplicity that it puzzled most men. It looked like the coarsest kind of sacking, had no ornamentation of any kind, and no apparent fastening or seams. But women knew better. Even the provincial old dears in Bertram's knew, quite certainly, that it had cost the earth!

Striding across the lounge towards the elevator, she passed quite close to Lady Selina and Miss Marple, and she nodded to the former.

"Hello, Lady Selina. Haven't seen you since Crufts. How are the borzois?"

"What on earth are you doing here, Bess?"

"Just staying here. I've driven up from Land's End. Four hours and three quarters. Not bad."

"You'll kill yourself one of these days. Or someone else."

"Oh, I hope not."

"But why are you staying here?"

Bess Sedgwick threw a swift glance round. She seemed to see the point and acknowledge it with an ironic smile.

"Someone told me I ought to try it. I think they're right. I've just had the most marvellous doughnut."

"My dear, they have real muffins too."

"Muffins," said Lady Sedgwick thoughtfully. "Yes. . . ." She seemed to concede the point. "Muffins!"

She nodded and went on towards the elevator.

"Extraordinary girl," said Lady Selina. To her, like to Miss Marple, every woman under sixty was a girl. "Known her ever since she was a child. Nobody could do anything with her. Ran away with an Irish groom when she was sixteen. They managed to get her back in time—or perhaps not in time. Anyway they bought him off and got her safely married to old Coniston—thirty years older than she was, awful old rip, quite dotty about her. That didn't last long. She went off with Johnnie Sedgwick. That might have stuck if he hadn't broken his neck steeplechasing. After that she married Ridgway Becker, the American yacht owner. He divorced her three years ago and I hear she's taken up with some racing-car driver—a Pole or something. I don't know whether she's actually married him or not. After the American divorce she went back to calling herself Sedgwick. She goes about with the most extraordinary people. They say she takes drugs . . . I don't know, I'm sure."

"One wonders if she is happy," said Miss Marple.

Lady Selina, who had clearly never wondered anything of the kind, looked rather startled.

"She's got packets of money, I suppose," she said doubtfully. "Alimony and all that. Of course that isn't everything . . ."

"No, indeed."

"And she's usually got a man—or several men—in tow."

"Yes?"

"Of course when some women get to that age, that's all they want. . . . But somehow—"

She paused.

"No," said Miss Marple. "*I* don't think so either."

There were people who would have smiled in gentle derision at this pronouncement on the part of an old-fashioned old lady who could hardly be expected to be an authority on nymphomania, and indeed it was not a word that Miss Marple would have used—her own phrase would have been "always too fond of men." But Lady Selina accepted her opinion as a confirmation of her own.

"There have been a lot of men in her life," she pointed out.

"Oh yes, but I should say, wouldn't you, that men were an adventure to her, not a need?"

And would any woman, Miss Marple wondered, come to Bertram's Hotel for an assignation with a man? Bertram's was very definitely not that sort of place. But possibly that could be, to someone of Bess Sedgwick's disposition, the very reason for choosing it.

She sighed, looked up at the handsome grandfather clock decorously ticking in the corner, and rose with the careful effort of the rheumatic to her feet. She walked slowly towards the elevator. Lady Selina cast a glance around her and pounced upon an elderly gentleman of military appearance who was reading the *Spectator*.

"How nice to see you again. Er—it is General Arlington, isn't it?"

But with great courtesy the old gentleman declined being General Arlington. Lady Selina apologized, but was not unduly discomposed. She combined short sight with optimism and since the thing she enjoyed most was meeting old friends and acquaintances, she was always making this kind of mistake. Many other people did the same, since the lights were pleasantly dim and heavily shaded. But nobody ever took offense—usually indeed it seemed to give them pleasure.

Miss Marple smiled to herself as she waited for the elevator to come down. So like Selina! Always convinced that she knew everybody. She herself could not compete. Her solitary achievement in that line had been the handsome and well-gaitered Bishop of Westchester whom she had addressed affectionately as "dear Robbie" and who had responded with equal affection and with memories of himself as a child in a Hampshire vicarage calling out lustily, "Be a crocodile now, Aunty Janie. Be a crocodile and eat me."

The elevator came down, the uniformed middle-aged man threw open the door. Rather to Miss Marple's surprise the alighting passenger was Bess Sedgwick whom she had seen go up only a minute or two before.

And then, one foot poised, Bess Sedgwick stopped dead, with a suddenness that surprised Miss Marple and made her own forward step falter. Bess Sedgwick was staring over Miss Marple's shoulder with such concentration that the old lady turned her own head.

The commissionaire had just pushed open the two swing doors of the entrance and was holding them to let two women pass through into the lounge. One of them was a fussy-looking middle-aged lady wearing a rather unfortunate flowered violet hat, the other was a tall, simply but smartly dressed girl of perhaps seventeen or eighteen with long straight flaxen hair.

Bess Sedgwick pulled herself together, wheeled round abruptly and re-entered the elevator. As Miss Marple followed her in, she turned to her and apologized.

"I'm so sorry. I nearly ran into you." She had a warm friendly voice. "I just remembered I'd forgotten something—which sounds nonsense but isn't really."

"Second floor?" said the operator. Miss Marple smiled and nodded in acknowledgment of the apology, got out and walked slowly along to her room, pleasurably turning over sundry little unimportant problems in her mind as was so often her custom.

For instance what Lady Sedgwick had said wasn't true. She had only just gone up to her room, and it must have been then that she "remembered she had forgotten something" (if there had been any truth in that statement at all) and had come down to find it. Or had she perhaps come down to meet someone or look for someone? But if so, what she had seen as the elevator door opened had startled and upset her, and she had immediately swung round into the elevator again and gone up so as not to meet whoever it was she had seen.

It must have been the two newcomers. The middle-aged woman and the girl. Mother and daughter? No, Miss Marple thought, *not* mother and daughter.

Even at Bertram's, thought Miss Marple, happily, interesting things could happen. . . .

3

"Er—is Colonel Luscombe—?"

The woman in the violet hat was at the desk. Miss
Gorringe smiled in a welcoming manner and a page,
who had been standing at the ready, was immediately
dispatched but had no need to fulfil his errand, as
Colonel Luscombe himself entered the lounge at that
moment and came quickly across to the desk.

"How do you do, Mrs. Carpenter." He shook hands
politely, then turned to the girl. "My dear Elvira." He
took both her hands affectionately in his. "Well, well,
this *is* nice. Splendid—splendid. Come and let's sit
down." He led them to chairs, established them. "Well,
well," he repeated, "this is nice."

The effort he made was somewhat palpable as was
his lack of ease. He could hardly go on saying how nice
this was. The two ladies were not very helpful. Elvira
smiled very sweetly. Mrs. Carpenter gave a meaning-
less little laugh, and smoothed her gloves.

"A good journey, eh?"

"Yes, thank you," said Elvira.

"No fog. Nothing like that?"

"Oh no."

"Our flight was five minutes ahead of time," said Mrs. Carpenter.

"Yes, yes. Good, very good." He took a pull upon himself. "I hope this place will be all right for you?"

"Oh, I'm sure it's very nice," said Mrs. Carpenter warmly, glancing round her. "Very comfortable."

"Rather old-fashioned, I'm afraid," said the colonel apologetically. "Rather a lot of old fogies. No—er—dancing, anything like that."

"No, I suppose not," agreed Elvira.

She glanced round in an expressionless manner. It certainly seemed impossible to connect Bertram's with dancing.

"Lot of old fogies here, I'm afraid," said Colonel Luscombe repeating himself. "Ought, perhaps, to have taken you somewhere more modern. Not very well up in these things, you see."

"This is very nice," said Elvira politely.

"It's only for a couple of nights," went on Colonel Luscombe. "I thought we'd go to a show this evening. A musical—" he said the word rather doubtfully, as though not sure he was using the right term. *Let Down Your Hair, Girls. I hope that will be all right?"

"How delightful," exclaimed Mrs. Carpenter. "That will be a treat, won't it, Elvira?"

"Lovely," said Elvira, tonelessly.

"And then supper afterwards? At the Savoy?"

Fresh exclamations from Mrs. Carpenter. Colonel Luscombe, stealing a glance at Elvira, cheered up a little. He thought that Elvira was pleased, though quite determined to express nothing more than polite approval in front of Mrs. Carpenter. "And I don't blame her," he said to himself.

He said to Mrs. Carpenter, "Perhaps you'd like to see your rooms—see they're all right and all that—"

"Oh, I'm sure they will be."

"Well, if there's anything you don't like about them, we'll make them change it. They know me here very well."

Miss Gorringe, in charge at the desk, was pleasantly welcoming. Nos. 28 and 29 on the second floor with an adjoining bathroom.

"I'll go up and get things unpacked," said Mrs. Carpenter. "Perhaps, Elvira, you and Colonel Luscombe would like to have a little gossip."

Tact, thought Colonel Luscombe. A bit obvious, perhaps, but anyway it would get rid of her for a bit. Though what he was going to gossip about to Elvira, he really didn't know. A very nice-mannered girl, but he wasn't used to girls. His wife had died in childbirth and the baby, a boy, had been brought up by his wife's family while an elder sister had come to keep house for him. His son had married and gone to live in Kenya, and his grandchildren were eleven, five, and two and a half and had been entertained on their last visit by football and space science talk, electric trains, and a ride on his foot. Easy! But young girls!

He asked Elvira if she would like a drink. He was about to propose a bitter lemon, ginger ale, or orangeade, but Elvira forestalled him.

"Thank you. I should like a gin and vermouth."

Colonel Luscombe looked at her rather doubtfully. He supposed girls of—what was she?—sixteen? seventeen?—did drink gin and vermouth. But he reassured himself that Elvira knew, so to speak, correct Greenwich social time. He ordered a gin and vermouth and a dry sherry.

He cleared his throat and asked, "How was Italy?"

"Very nice, thank you."

"And that place you were at, the Contessa what's-her-name? Not too grim?"

"She is rather strict. But I didn't let that worry me."

He looked at her, not quite sure whether the reply was not slightly ambiguous.

He said, stammering a little, but with a more natural manner than he had been able to manage before:

"I'm afraid we don't know each other as well as we ought to, seeing I'm your guardian as well as your god-father. Difficult for me, you know—difficult for a man who's an old buffer like me—to know what a girl wants—at least—I mean to know what a girl ought to have. Schools and then after schools—what they used to call finishing in my day. But now, I suppose it's all more serious. Careers, eh? Jobs? All that? We'll have to have a talk about all that sometime. Anything in particular you want to do"

"I suppose I shall take a secretarial course," said Elvira without enthusiasm.

"Oh. You want to be a secretary?"

"Not particularly."

"Oh—well, then—"

"It's just what you start with," Elvira explained.

Colonel Luscombe had an odd feeling of being relegated to his place.

"These cousins of mine, the Melfords. You think you'll like living with them? If not—"

"Oh, I think so. I like Nancy quite well. And Cousin Mildred is rather a dear."

"That's all right then?"

"Quite, for the present."

Luscombe did not know what to say to that. While he was considering what next to say, Elvira spoke. Her words were simple and direct. "Have I any money?"

Again he took his time before answering, studying her thoughtfully. Then he said, "Yes. You've got quite a lot of money. That is to say, you will have when you are twenty-one."

"Who has got it now?"

He smiled. "It's held in trust for you; a certain amount is deducted each year from the income to pay for your maintenance and education."

"And you are the trustee?"

"One of them. There are three."

"What happens if I die?"

"Come, come, Elvira, you're not going to die. What nonsense!"

"I hope not—but one never knows, does one? An airliner crashed only last week and everyone was killed."

"Well, it's not going to happen to you," said Luscombe firmly.

"You can't really know that," said Elvira. "I was just wondering who would get my money if I died?"

"I haven't the least idea," said the colonel irritably. "Why do you ask?"

"It might be interesting," said Elvira thoughtfully. "I wondered if it would be worth anyone's while to kill me."

"Really, Elvira! This is a most unprofitable conversation. I can't understand why your mind dwells on such things."

"Oh. Just ideas. One wants to know what the facts really are."

"You're not thinking of the Mafia—or something like that?"

"Oh no. That would be silly. Who would get my money if I was married?"

"Your husband, I suppose. But really—"

34

"Are you sure of that?"

"No, I'm not in the least sure. It depends on the wording of the trust. But you're not married, so why worry?"

Elvira did not reply. She seemed lost in thought. Finally she came out of her trance and asked:

"Do you ever see my mother?"

"Sometimes. Not very often."

"Where is she now?"

"Oh—abroad."

"Where abroad?"

"France—Portugal. I don't really know."

"Does she ever want to see me?"

Her limpid gaze met his. He didn't know what to reply. Was this a moment for truth? Or for vagueness? Or for a good thumping lie? What could you say to a girl who asked a question of such simplicity, when the answer was of great complexity?

"I don't know," he said unhappily.

Her eyes searched him gravely. Luscombe felt throughly ill at ease. He was making a mess of this. The girl must wonder—clearly was wondering. Any girl would.

He said, "You mustn't think—I mean it's difficult to explain. Your mother is, well, rather different from—" Elvira was nodding energetically.

"I know. I'm always reading about her in the papers. She's something rather special, isn't she? In fact, she's rather a wonderful person."

"Yes," agreed the colonel. "That's exactly right. She's a wonderful person." He paused and then went on. "But a wonderful person is very often—" He stopped and started again. "It's not always a happy thing to have a wonderful person for a mother. You can take that from me because it's the truth."

"You don't like speaking the truth very much, do you? But I think what you've just said *is* the truth."

They both sat staring towards the big brass bound swing doors that led to the world outside.

Suddenly the doors were pushed open with violence —a violence quite unusual in Bertram's Hotel—and a young man strode in and went straight across to the desk. He wore a black leather jacket. His vitality was such that Bertram's Hotel took on the atmosphere of a museum by way of contrast. The people were the dust-encrusted relics of a past age. He bent towards Miss Gorringe.

"Is Lady Sedgwick staying here?" he asked.

Miss Gorringe on this occasion had no welcoming smile. Her eyes were flinty.

"Yes," she said. Then, with definite unwillingness, she stretched out her hands towards the telephone. "Do you want to—?"

"No," said the young man. "I just wanted to leave a note for her."

He produced it from a pocket of his leather coat and slid it across the mahogany counter.

"I only wanted to be sure this was the right hotel."

There might have been some slight incredulity in his voice as he looked round him, then turned back towards the entrance. His eyes passed indifferently over the people sitting round him. They passed over Luscombe and Elvira in the same way, and Luscombe felt a sudden unsuspected anger. Dammit all, he thought to himself, Elvira's a pretty girl. When I was a young chap I'd have noticed a pretty girl, especially among all these fossils. But the young man seemed to have no interested eyes to spare for pretty girls. He turned back to the desk and asked, raising his voice slightly as though to call Miss Gorringe's attention.

"What's the telephone number here—1129, isn't it?"

"No," said Miss Gorringe, "3925."

"Regent?"

"No. Mayfair."

He nodded. Then swiftly he strode across to the door and passed out, swinging the doors to behind him with something of the same explosive quality he had shown on entering.

Everybody seemed to draw a deep breath; to find difficulty in resuming their interrupted conversations.

"Well," said Colonel Luscombe, rather inadequately, as if at a loss for words. "Well, really! These young fellows nowadays. . . ."

Elvira was smiling.

"You recognized him, didn't you?" she said. "You know who he is?" She spoke in a slightly awed voice. She proceeded to enlighten him. "Ladislaus Malinowski."

"Oh, that chap." The name was indeed faintly familiar to Colonel Luscombe. "Racing driver."

"Yes. He was world champion two years running. He had a bad crash a year ago. Broke lots of things. But I believe he's driving again now." She raised her head to listen. "That's a racing car he's driving now."

The roar of the engine had penetrated through to Bertram's Hotel from the street outside. Colonel Luscombe perceived that Ladislaus Malinowski was one of Elvira's heroes. Well, he thought to himself, better that than one of those pop singers or crooners or long-haired Beatles or whatever they called themselves. Luscombe was old-fashioned in his views of young men.

The swing doors opened again. Both Elvira and Colonel Luscombe looked at them expectantly but Bertram's Hotel had reverted to normal. It was merely a white-haired elderly cleric who came in. He stood for a moment looking round him with a slightly puzzled air as of one who fails to understand where he was or how he had come there. Such an experience was no novelty to Canon Pennyfather. It came to him in trains when he did not remember where he had come from, where he was going, or why! It came to him when he was walking along the street, it came to him when he found himself sitting on a committee. It had come to him before now when he was in his cathedral stall, and did not know whether he had already preached his sermon or was about to do so.

"I believe I know that old boy," said Luscombe, peering at him. "Who is he now?" Stays here fairly often, I believe. Abercrombie? Archdeacon Abercrombie—no, it's not Abercrombie, though he's rather like Abercrombie."

Elvira glanced round at Canon Pennyfather without interest. Compared with a racing driver he had no appeal at all. She was not interested in ecclesiastics of any kind although, since being in Italy, she admitted to a mild admiration for cardinals whom she considered as at any rate properly picturesque.

Canon Pennyfather's face cleared and he nodded his head appreciatively. He had recognized where he was. In Bertram's Hotel, of course; where he was going to spend the night on his way to—now where was he on his way to? Chadminster? No, no, he had just come from Chadminster. He was going to—of course—to the Congress at Lucerne. He stepped forward, beaming, to the reception desk and was greeted warmly by Miss Gorringe.

"So glad to see you, Canon Pennyfather. How well you are looking."

"Thank you—thank you—I had a severe cold last

38

week but I've got over it now. You have a room for me. I *did* write?"

Miss Gorringe reassured him.

"Oh yes, Canon Pennyfather, we got your letter. We've reserved No. Nineteen for you, the room you had last time."

"Thank you—thank you. For—let me see—I shall want it for four days. Actually I am going to Lucerne and shall be away for one night, but please keep the room. I shall leave most of my things here and only take a small bag to Switzerland. There won't be any difficulty over that?"

Again Miss Gorringe reassured him. "Everything's going to be quite all right. You explained very clearly in your letter."

Other people might not have used the word "clearly." "Fully" would have been better, since he had certainly written at length.

All anxieties set at rest, Canon Pennyfather breathed a sigh of relief and was conveyed, together with his baggage, to Room 19.

In Room 28 Mrs. Carpenter had removed her crown of violets from her head and was carefully adjusting her nightdress on the pillow of her bed. She looked up as Elvira entered.

"Ah, there you are, my dear. Would you like me to help you with your unpacking?"

"No, thank you," said Elvira politely. "I shan't unpack very much, you know."

"Which of the bedrooms would you like to have? The bathroom is between them. I told them to put your luggage in the far one. I thought this room might be a little noisy."

"That was very kind of you," said Elvira in her expressionless voice.

"You're sure you wouldn't like me to help you?"

"No, thanks, really I wouldn't. I think I might perhaps have a bath."

"Yes, I think that's a very good idea. Would you like to have the first bath? I'd rather finish putting my things away."

Elvira nodded. She went into the adjoining bathroom, shut the door behind her and pushed the bolts across. She went into her own room, opened her suitcase and flung a few things on the bed. Then she undressed, put on a dressing gown, went into the bathroom and turned the taps on. She went back into her own room and sat down on the bed by the telephone. She listened a moment or two in case of interruptions, then lifted the receiver.

"This is Room Twenty-nine. Can you give me Regent 1129, please?"

4

Within the confines of Scotland Yard a conference was in progress. It was by way of being an informal conference. Six or seven men were sitting easily around a table and each of those six men was a man of some importance in his own line. The subject that occupied the attention of these guardians of the law was a subject that had grown terrifically in importance during the last two or three years. It concerned a branch of crime whose success had been overwhelmingly disquieting. Robbery on a big scale was increasing. Bank holdups, snatches of payrolls, thefts of consignments of jewels sent through the mail, train robberies. Hardly a month passed but some daring and stupendous coup was attempted and brought off successfully.

Sir Ronald Graves, Assistant Commissioner of Scotland Yard, was presiding at the head of the table. According to his usual custom he did more listening than talking. No formal reports were being presented on this occasion. All that belonged to the ordinary routine of C.I.D. work. This was a high-level consultation, a general pooling of ideas between men looking at affairs from slightly different points of view. Sir Ronald Graves's eyes went slowly round his little group, then he nodded his head to a man at the end of the table.

"Well, Father," he said, "let's hear a few homely wisecracks from you."

The man addressed as "Father" was Chief Inspector Fred Davy. His retirement lay not long ahead and he appeared to be even more elderly than he was. Hence his nickname of Father. He had a comfortable spreading presence, and such a benign and kindly manner that many criminals had been disagreeably surprised to find him a less genial and gullible man than he had seemed to be.

"Yes, Father, let's hear your views," said another Chief Inspector.

"It's big," said Chief Inspector Davy with a deep sigh. "Yes, it's big. Maybe it's growing."

"When you say big, do you mean numerically?"

"Yes, I do."

Another man, Comstock, with a sharp, foxy face and alert eyes, broke in to say,

"Would you say that was an advantage to them?"

"Yes and no," said Father. "It could be a disaster. But so far, devil take it, they've got it all well under control."

Superintendent Andrews, a fair, slight, dreamy-looking man, said thoughtfully:

"I've always thought there's a lot more to size than people realize. Take a little one-man business. If that's well run and if it's the right size, it's a sure and certain winner. Branch out, make it bigger, increase personnel, and perhaps you'll get it suddenly to the wrong size and down the hill it goes. The same way with a great big chain of stores. An empire in industry. If that's big enough it will succeed. If it's not big enough it just won't manage it. Everything has got its right size. When it is its right size and well run it's the tops."

"How big do you think this show is?" Sir Ronald barked.

"Bigger than we thought at first," said Comstock.

A tough-looking man, Inspector McNeill, said, "It's growing, I'd say. Father's right. Growing all the time."

"That may be a good thing," said Davy. "It may grow a bit too fast, and then it'll get out of hand."

"The question is, Sir Ronald," said McNeill, "who we pull in and when?"

"There's a round dozen or so we could pull in," said Comstock. "The Harris lot are mixed up in it, we know that. There's a nice little pocket down Luton way. There's a garage at Epsom, there's a pub near Maidenhead, and there's a farm on the Great North Road."

"Any of them worth pulling in?"

"I don't think so. Small fry all of them. Links. Just links here and there in the chain. A spot where cars are converted, and turned over quickly; a respectable pub where messages get passed; a secondhand clothes shop where appearance can be altered, a theatrical costumer in the East End, also very useful. They're paid, these people. Quite well paid but they don't really know anything!"

The dreamy Superintendent Andrews said again, "We're up against some good brains. We haven't got near them yet. We know some of their affiliations and that's all. As I say, the Harris crowd are in it and Marks is in on the financial end. The foreign contacts are in touch with Weber but he's only an agent. We've nothing actually on any of these people. We know that they all have ways of maintaining contact with each other, and with the different branches of the concern, but we don't know exactly how they do it. We watch them and follow them, and they know we're watching them. Somewhere there's a great central exchange. What we want to get at is the planners."

"It's like a giant network," Comstock said. "I agree that there must be an operational headquarters somewhere. A place where each operation is planned and detailed and dovetailed completely. Somewhere, someone plots it all, and produces a working blueprint of Operation Mailbag or Operation Payroll. Those are the people we're out to get."

"Possibly they are not even in this country," said Father quietly.

"No, I dare say that's true. Perhaps they're in an igloo somewhere, or in a tent in Morocco or in a chalet in Switzerland."

"I don't believe in these masterminds," said McNeill shaking his head. "They sound all right in a story. There's got to be a head, of course, but I don't believe in a master criminal. I'd say there was a very clever little board of directors behind this. Centrally planned, with a chairman. They've got on to something good, and they're improving their technique all the time. All the same—"

"Yes?" said Sir Ronald encouragingly.

"Even in a right tight little team, there are probably expendables. What I call the Russian sledge principle. From time to time, if they think we might be getting hot on the scent, they throw off one of them, the one they think they can best afford."

"Would they dare to do that? Wouldn't it be rather risky?"

"I'd say it could be done in such a way that whoever it was wouldn't even know he had been pushed off the sledge. He'd just think he'd fallen off. He'd keep quiet because he'd think it was worth his while to keep quiet. So it would be, of course. They've got plenty of money to play with, and they can afford to be generous. Family looked after, if he's got one, while he's in prison. Possibly an escape engineered."

"There's been too much of that," said Comstock.

"I think, you know," said Sir Ronald, "that it's not much good going over and over our speculations again. We always say much the same thing."

McNeill laughed.

"What is it you really wanted us for, sir?"

"Well—" Sir Ronald thought a moment, "we're all agreed on the main things," he said slowly. "We're all agreed on our main policy, what we're trying to do. I think it might be profitable to have a look around for some of the small things, the things that don't matter much, that are just a bit out of the usual run. It's hard to explain what I mean, but like that business some years ago in the Culver case. An ink stain. Do you remember? An ink stain round a mousehole. Now why on earth should a man empty a bottle of ink into a mousehole? It didn't seem important. It was hard to get at the answer. But when we did hit on the answer, it led somewhere. That's—roughly—the sort of thing I was thinking about. Odd things. Don't mind saying if you come across something that strikes you as a bit out of the usual. Petty if you like, but irritating, because it doesn't quite fit in. I see Father's nodding his head."

"Couldn't agree with you more," said Chief Inspector Davy. "Come on, boys, try to come up with something. Even if it's only a man wearing a funny hat."

There was no immediate response. Everyone looked a little uncertain and doubtful.

"Come on," said Father, "I'll stick my neck out first. It's just a funny story, really, but you might as well have it for what it's worth. The London and Metropolitan Bank holdup. Carmolly Street Branch. Remember it? A whole list of car numbers and car colours and makes. We appealed to people to come forward and they responded—how they responded! About a hundred and fifty pieces of misleading information! Got it sorted out in the end to about seven cars that had been seen in the neighbourhood, any one of which might have been concerned in the robbery."

"Yes," said Sir Ronald, "go on."

"There were one or two we couldn't get tags on. Looked as though the numbers might have been changed. Nothing out of the way in that. It's often done. Most of them got tracked down in the end. I'll just bring up one instance. Morris Oxford, black saloon, number CMG 256, reported by a probation officer. He said it was being driven my Mr. Justice Ludgrove."

He looked round. They were listening to him, but without any manifest interest.

"I know," he said, "wrong as usual. Mr. Justice Ludgrove is a rather noticeable old boy, ugly as sin for one thing. Well, it wasn't Mr. Ludgrove because at that exact time he was actually in Court. He has got a Morris Oxford, but its number isn't CMG 256." He looked round. "All right. All right. So there's no point in it, you'll say. But do you know what the number was? CMG 265. Near enough, eh? Just the sort of mistake one does make when you're trying to remember a car number."

"I'm sorry," said Sir Ronald, "I don't quite see—"

"No," said Chief Inspector Davy, "there's nothing to see really, is there? Only—it was very like the actual car number, wasn't it? 265——256 CMG. Really rather a coincidence that there should be a Morris

46

Oxford car of the right colour with the number just one digit wrong, and with a man in it closely resembling the owner of the car."

"Do you mean—?"

"Just one little digit difference. Today's 'deliberate mistake.' It almost seems like that."

"Sorry, Davy. I still don't get it."

"Oh, I don't suppose there's anything to get. There's a Morris Oxford car, CMG 265, proceeding along the street two and half minutes after the bank snatch. In it, the probation officer recognizes Mr. Justice Ludgrove."

"Are you suggesting it really was Mr. Justice Ludgrove? Come now, Davy."

"No, I'm not suggesting that it was Mr. Justice Ludgrove and that he was mixed up in a bank robbery. He was staying at Bertram's Hotel in Pond Street, and he was at the Law Courts at that exact time. All proved up to the hilt. I'm saying the car number and make and the identification by a probation officer who knows old Ludgrove quite well by sight is the kind of coincidence that ought to mean something. Apparently it doesn't. Too bad."

Comstock stirred uneasily. "There was another case a bit like that in connection with the jewellery business at Brighton. Some old admiral or other. I've forgotten his name now. Some woman identified him most positively as having been on the scene."

"And he wasn't?"

"No, he'd been in London that night. Went up for some naval dinner or other, I think."

"Staying at his club?"

"No, he was staying at a hotel—I believe it was that one you mentioned just now, Father, Bertram's, isn't it? Quiet place. A lot of old service geezers go there, I believe."

"Bertram's Hotel," said Chief Inspector Davy thoughtfully.

5

Miss Marple awoke early because she always woke early. She was appreciative of her bed. Most comfortable.

She pattered across to the window and pulled the curtains, admitting a little pallid London daylight. As yet, however, she did not try to dispense with the electric light. A very nice bedroom they had given her, again quite in the tradition of Bertram's. A rose-flowered wallpaper, a large well-polished mahogany chest of drawers—a dressing table to correspond. Two upright chairs, one easy chair of a reasonable height from the ground. A connecting door led to a bathroom which was modern but which had a tiled wallpaper of roses and so avoided any suggestion of overfrigid hygiene.

Miss Marple got back into bed, plumped her pillows up, glanced at her clock, half-past seven, picked up the small devotional book that always accompanied her, and read as usual the page and a half allotted to the day. Then she picked up her knitting and began to knit, slowly at first, since her fingers were stiff and rheumatic when she first awoke, but very soon her pace grew faster, and her fingers lost their painful stiffness.

"Another day," said Miss Marple to herself, greeting the fact with her usual gentle pleasure. Another day —and who knew what it might bring forth?

She relaxed, and abandoning her knitting, let thoughts pass in an idle stream through her head. . . . Selina Hazy . . . what a pretty cottage she had had in St. Mary Mead's—and now someone had put on that ugly green roof. . . . Muffins . . . very wasteful in butter . . . but very good. . . . And fancy serving old-fashioned seed cake! She had never expected, not for a moment, that things would be as much like they used to be . . . because, after all, Time didn't stand still. . . . And to have made it stand still in this way must really have cost a lot of money. . . . Not a bit of plastic in the place! . . . It must pay them, she supposed. The out-of-date returns in due course as the picturesque. . . . Look how people wanted old-fashioned roses now, and scorned hybrid teas! . . . None of this place seemed real at all. . . . Well, why should it? . . . It was fifty—no, nearer sixty years since she had stayed here. And it didn't seem real to her because she was now acclimatized in this present year of Our Lord. Really, the whole thing opened up a very interesting set of problems. . . . The atmosphere and the people. . . . Miss Marple's fingers pushed her knitting farther away from her.

"Pockets," she said aloud. . . . "Pockets, I suppose. . . . And quite difficult to find. . . ."

Would that account for that curious feeling of uneasiness she had had last night? That feeling that something was wrong. . . .

All those elderly people—really very much like those she remembered when she had stayed here fifty years ago. They had been natural then—but they weren't very natural now. Elderly people nowadays weren't like elderly people then—they had that worried harried look of domestic anxieties with which they are too tired to cope, or they rushed around to committees and tried to appear bustling and competent, or they dyed their hair gentian blue, or wore wigs, and their hands were not the hands she remembered, tapering, delicate hands—they were harsh from washing up and detergents. . . .

And so—well, so these people didn't look real. But the point was that they were real. Selina Hazy was real. And that rather handsome old military man in the corner was real—she had met him once, although she did not recall his name—and the Bishop (dear Robbie!) was dead.

Miss Marple glanced at her little clock. It was eight-thirty. Time for her breakfast.

She examined the instructions given by the hotel—splendid big print so that it wasn't necessary to put one's spectacles on.

Meals could be ordered through the telephone by asking for room service, or you could press the bell labelled Chambermaid.

Miss Marple did the latter. Talking to room service always flustered her.

The result was excellent. In no time at all there was a tap on the door and a highly satisfactory chambermaid appeared. A real chambermaid looking unreal, wearing a striped lavender print dress and actually a cap, a freshly laundered cap. A smiling, rosy positively countrified face. Where did they find these people?

Miss Marple ordered her breakfast. Tea, poached eggs, fresh rolls. So adept was the chambermaid that she did not even mention cereals or orange juice.

Five minutes later breakfast came. A comfortable tray with a big pot-bellied teapot, creamy-looking milk, a silver hot water jug. Two beautifully poached eggs on toast, poached the proper way, not little round hard bullets shaped in tin cups, a good-sized round of butter stamped with a thistle. Marmalade, honey, and strawberry jam. Delicious-looking rolls, not the hard kind with papery interiors—they smelled of fresh bread (the most delicious smell in the world!). There were also an apple, a pear, and a banana.

Miss Marple inserted a knife gingerly but with confidence. She was not disappointed. Rich deep yellow yolk oozed out, thick and creamy. Proper eggs!

Everything piping hot. A real breakfast. She could have cooked it herself but she hadn't had to! It was brought to her as if—no, not as though she were a queen—as though she were a middle-aged lady staying in a good but not unduly expensive hotel. In fact —back to 1909. Miss Marple expressed appreciation to the chambermaid who replied smiling, "Oh, yes, madam, the chef is very particular about his breakfasts."

Miss Marple studied her appraisingly. Bertram's Hotel could certainly produce marvels. A real housemaid. She pinched her left arm surreptitiously.

"Have you been here long?" she asked.

"Just over three years, madam."

"And before that?"

"I was in a hotel at Eastbourne. Very modern and up-to-date—but I prefer an old-fashioned place like this."

Miss Marple took a sip of tea. She found herself humming in a vague way—words fitting themselves to a long-forgotten song. *"Oh, where have you been all my life. . . ."*

The chambermaid was looking slightly startled.

"I was just remembering an old song," twittered Miss Marple apologetically. "Very popular at one time."

Again she sang softly. "Oh where have you been all my life. . . ."

"Perhaps you know it?" she asked.

"Well—" The chambermaid looked rather apologetic.

"Too long ago for you," said Miss Marple. "Ah well, one gets to remembering things—in a place like this."

"Yes, madam, a lot of the ladies who stay here feel like that, I think."

"It's partly why they come, I expect," said Miss Marple.

The chambermaid went out. She was obviously used to old ladies who twittered and reminisced.

Miss Marple finished her breakfast, and got up in a pleasant leisurely fashion. She had a plan ready made for a delightful morning of shopping. Not too much— to overtire herself. Oxford Street today, perhaps. And tomorrow Knightsbridge. She planned ahead happily.

It was about ten o'clock when she emerged from her room fully equipped: hat, gloves, umbrella—just in case, though it looked fine—handbag—her smartest shopping bag.

The door next but one on the corridor opened sharply and someone looked out. It was Bess Sedgwick. She withdrew back into the room and closed the door sharply.

Miss Marple wondered as she went down the stairs. She preferred the stairs to the elevator first thing in the morning. It limbered her up. Her steps grew slower and slower . . . she stopped.

II

As Colonel Luscombe strode along the passage from his room, a door at the top of the stairs opened sharply and Lady Sedgwick spoke to him.

"There you are at last! I've been on the lookout for you—waiting to pounce. Where can we go and talk? This is to say without falling over some old pussy every second."

"Well, really, Bess, I'm not quite sure—I think on the mezzanine floor there's a sort of writing room."

"You'd better come in here. Quick now, before the chambermaid gets peculiar ideas about us."

Rather unwillingly, Colonel Luscombe stepped across the threshold and had the door shut firmly behind him.

"I'd no idea you would be staying here, Bess. I hadn't the faintest idea of it."

"I don't suppose you had."

"I mean—I would never have brought Elvira here. I *have* got Elvira here, you know?"

"Yes, I saw her with you last night."

"But I really didn't know that you were here. It seemed such an unlikely place for you."

"I don't see why," said Bess Sedgwick coldly. "It's far and away the most comfortable hotel in London. Why shouldn't I stay here?"

"You must understand that I hadn't any idea of . . . I mean—"

She looked at him and laughed. She was dressed ready to go out in a well-cut dark suit and a shirt of bright emerald green. She looked gay and very much alive. Beside her, Colonel Luscombe looked rather old and faded.

"Darling Derek, don't look so worried. I'm not accusing you of trying to stage a mother and daughter sentimental meeting. It's just one of those things that happen; where people meet each other in unsuspected places. But you must get Elvira out of here, Derek. You must get her out of here at once—today."

"Oh, she's going. I mean, I only brought her here just for a couple of nights. Do a show—that sort of thing. She's going down to the Melfords tomorrow."

"Poor girl, that'll be boring for her."

Luscombe looked at her with concern. "Do you think she will be very bored?"

Bess took pity on him.

"Probably not after duress in Italy. She might even think it wildly thrilling."

Luscombe took his courage in both hands.

"Look here, Bess, I was startled to find you here, but don't you think it—well, you know, it might be meant in a way. I mean that it might be an opportunity—I don't think you really know how—well, how the girl might feel."

"What are you trying to say, Derek?"

"Well, you are her mother, you know."

"Of course I'm her mother. She's my daughter. And what good has that fact ever been to either of us, or ever will be?"

"You can't be sure. I think—I think she feels it."

"What gives you that idea?" said Bess Sedgwick sharply.

"Something she said yesterday. She asked where you were, what you were doing."

Bess Sedgwick walked across the room to the window. She stood there a moment tapping on the pane.

"You're so nice, Derek," she said. "You have such nice ideas. But they don't work, my poor angel. That's what you've got to say to yourself. They don't work and they might be dangerous."

"Oh, come now, Bess. Dangerous?"

"Yes, yes, yes. Dangerous. I'm dangerous. I've always been dangerous."

"When I think of some of the things you've done," said Colonel Luscombe.

"That's my own business," said Bess Sedgwick. "Running into danger has become a kind of habit with me. No, I wouldn't say habit. More an addiction. Like a drug. Like that nice little dollop of heroin addicts have to have every so often to make life seem bright coloured and worth living. Well, that's all right. That's my funeral—or not—as the case may be. I've never taken drugs—never needed them. Danger has been my drug. But people who live as I do can be a source of harm to others. Now don't be an obstinate old fool, Derek. You keep that girl well away from me. I can do her no good. Only harm. If possible, don't even let her know I was staying in the same hotel. Ring up the Melfords and take her down there today. Make some excuse about a sudden emergency—"

Colonel Luscombe hesitated, pulling his moustache.

"I think you're making a mistake, Bess." He sighed. "She asked where you were. I told her you were abroad."

"Well, I shall be in another twelve hours, so that all fits very nicely."

She came up to him, kissed him on the point of his chin, turned him smartly around as though they were about to play blind man's buff, opened the door, gave him a gentle little propelling shove out of it. As the door shut behind him, Colonel Luscombe noticed an old lady turning the corner from the stairs. She was muttering to herself as she looked into her handbag. "Dear, dear me. I suppose I must have left it in my room. Oh dear."

She passed Colonel Luscombe without paying much attention to him apparently, but as he went on down the stairs Miss Marple paused by her room door and directed a piercing glance after him. Then she looked towards Bess Sedgwick's door. "So that's who she was waiting for," said Miss Marple to herself. "I wonder why."

III

Canon Pennyfather, fortified by breakfast, wandered across the lounge, remembered to leave his key at the desk, pushed his way through the swinging doors, and was neatly inserted into a taxi by the Irish commissionaire who existed for this purpose.

"Where to, sir?"

"Oh dear," said Canon Pennyfather in sudden dismay. "Now let me see—where *was* I going?"

The traffic in Pond Street was held up for some minutes whilst Canon Pennyfather and the commissionaire debated this knotty point. Finally Canon Pennyfather had a brainwave and the taxi was directed to go to the British Museum.

The commissionaire was left on the pavement with a broad grin on his face, and since no other exits seemed to be taking place, he strolled a little way along the façade of the hotel whistling an old tune in a muted manner.

One of the windows on the ground floor of Bertram's was flung up—but the commissionaire did not even turn his head until a voice spoke unexpectedly through the open window.

"So this is where you've landed up, Micky. What on earth brought you to this place?"

He swung round, startled—and stared.

Lady Sedgwick thrust her head through the open window.

"Don't you know me?" she demanded.

A sudden gleam of recognition came across the man's face.

"Why, if it isn't little Bessie now! Fancy that! After all these years. Little Bessie."

"Nobody but you ever called me Bessie. It's a revolting name. What have you been doing all these years?"

"This and that," said Micky with some reserve. "I've not been in the news like you have. I've read of your doings in the paper time and again."

Bess Sedgwick laughed. "Anyway, I've worn better than you have," she said. "You drink too much. You always did."

"You've worn well because you've always been in the money."

"Money wouldn't have done you any good. You'd have drunk even more and gone to the dogs completely. Oh yes, you would! What brought you here? That's what I want to know. How did you ever get taken on at this place?"

"I wanted a job. I had these—" his hand flicked over the row of medals.

"Yes, I see." She was thoughtful. "All genuine too, aren't they?"

"Sure they're genuine. Why shouldn't they be?"

"Oh I believe you. You always had courage. You've

58

always been a good fighter. Yes, the Army suited you. I'm sure of that."

"The Army's all right in time of war, but it's no good in peacetime."

"So you took to this stuff. I hadn't the least idea—" she stopped.

"You hadn't the least idea what, Bessie?"

"Nothing. It's queer seeing you again after all these years."

"I haven't forgotten," said the man. "I've never forgotten you, little Bessie. Ah, a lovely girl you were! A lovely slip of a girl."

"A damn fool of a girl, that's what I was," said Lady Sedgwick.

"That's true now. You hadn't much sense. If you had, you wouldn't have taken up with me. What hands you had for a horse. Do you remember that mare— what was her name now?—Molly O'Flynn. Ah, she was a wicked devil, that one was."

"You were the only one that could ride her," said Lady Sedgwick.

"She'd have had me off if she could! When she found she couldn't, she gave in. Ah, she was a beauty, now. But talking of sitting a horse, there wasn't one lady in those parts better than you. A lovely seat you had, lovely hands. Never any fear in you, not for a minute! And it's been the same ever since, so I judge. Aeroplanes, racing cars."

Bess Sedgwick laughed. "I must get on with my letters."

She drew back from the window.

Mickey leaned over the railing. "I've not forgotten Ballygowlan," he said with meaning. "Sometimes I've thought of writing to you—"

Bess Sedgwick's voice came out harshly. "And what do you mean by that, Mick Gorman?"

"I was just saying as I haven't forgotten—anything. I was just—reminding you like."

Bess Sedgwick's voice still held its harsh note. "If you mean what I think you mean, I'll give you a piece of advice. Any trouble from you, and I'd shoot you as easily as I'd shoot a rat. I've shot men before—"

"In foreign parts, maybe—"

"Foreign parts or here—it's all the same to me."

"Ah, good Lord, now, and I believe you would do just that!" His voice held admiration. "In Ballygowlan—"

"In Ballygowlan," she cut in, "they paid you to keep your mouth shut and paid you well. You took the money. You'll get no more from me so don't think it."

"It would be a nice romantic story for the Sunday papers. . . ."

"You heard what I said."

"Ah," he laughed, "I'm not serious, I was just joking. I'd never do anything to hurt my little Bessie. I'll keep my mouth shut."

"Mind you do," said Lady Sedgwick.

She shut down the window. Staring down at the desk in front of her she looked at her unfinished letter on the blotting paper. She picked it up, looked at it, crumpled it into a ball and flung it into the wastepaper basket. Then abruptly she got up from her seat and walked out of the room. She did not even cast a glance around her before she went.

The smaller writing rooms at Bertram's often had an appearance of being empty even when they were not. Two well-appointed desks stood in the windows, there was a table on the right that held a few magazines, on the left were two very high-backed armchairs turned towards the fire. These were favourite spots in the afternoon for elderly military or naval gentlemen to ensconce themselves and fall happily asleep until tea-time. Anyone coming in to write a letter did not usually even notice them. The chairs were not so much in demand during the morning.

As it happened, however, they were on this particular morning both occupied. An old lady was in one and a young girl in the other. The young girl rose to her feet. She stood a moment looking uncertainly towards the door through which Lady Sedgwick had passed out, then she moved slowly towards it. Elvira Blake's face was deadly pale.

It was another five minutes before the old lady moved. Then Miss Marple decided that the little rest which she always took after dressing and coming downstairs had lasted quite long enough. It was time to go out and enjoy the pleasures of London. She might walk as far as Piccadilly, and take a No. 9 bus to High Street, Kensington, or she might walk along to Bond Street and take a 25 bus to Marshall and Snelgrove's or she might take a 25 the other way which as far as she remembered would land her up at the Army and Navy Stores. Passing through the swing doors she was still savouring these delights in her mind. The Irish commissionaire, back on duty, made up her mind for her.

"You'll be wanting a taxi, ma'am," he said with firmness.

"I don't think I do," said Miss Marple. "I think there's a twenty-five bus I could take quite near here —or a two from Park Lane."

"You'll not be wanting a bus," said the commissionaire firmly. "It's very dangerous springing on a bus when you're getting on in life. The way they start and stop and go on again. Jerk you off your feet, they do. No heart at all, these fellows, nowadays. I'll whistle you along a taxi and you'll go to wherever you want to like a queen."

Miss Marple considered and fell.

"Very well then," she said, "perhaps I had better have a taxi."

The commissionaire had no need even to whistle. He merely clicked his thumb and a taxi appeared like magic. Miss Marple was helped into it with every possible care and decided on the spur of the moment to go to Robinson and Cleaver's and look at their splendid offer of real linen sheets. She sat happily in her taxi feeling indeed as the commissionaire had promised her, just like a queen. Her mind was filled with pleasurable anticipation of linen sheets, linen pillow cases, and proper dish and kitchen cloths without pictures of bananas, figs, or performing dogs and other pictorial distractions to annoy you when you were washing up.

Lady Sedgwick came up to the reception desk. "Mr. Humfries in his office?"

"Yes, Lady Sedgwick." Miss Gorringe looked startled.

Lady Sedgwick passed behind the desk, tapped on the door and went in without waiting for any response.

Mr. Humfries looked up. "What—"

"Who engaged that man Michael Gorman?"

Mr. Humfries spluttered a little.

"Parfitt left—he had a car accident a month ago. We had to replace him quickly. This man seemed all right. References O.K.— ex-Army—quite good record. Not very bright perhaps, but that's all the better sometimes. You don't know anything against him, do you?"

"Enough not to want him here."

"If you insist," Humfries said, "we'll give him his notice—"

"No," said Lady Sedgwick slowly. "No—it's too late for that. Never mind."

6

"Elvira."

"Hello, Bridget."

The Honourable Elvira Blake pushed her way through the front door of 180 Onslow Square, which her friend Bridget had rushed down to open for her, having been watching through the window.

"Let's go upstairs," said Elvira.

"Yes, we'd better. Otherwise we'll get entangled by Mummy."

The two girls rushed up the stairs, thereby circumventing Bridget's mother, who came out on to the landing from her own bedroom just too late.

"You really are lucky not to have a mother," said Bridget, rather breathlessly as she took her friend into her bedroom and shut the door firmly. "I mean, Mummy's quite a pet and all that, but the questions she asks! Morning, noon, and night. Where are you going, and who have you met? And are they cousins of somebody else of the same name in Yorkshire! I mean, the futility of it all."

"I suppose they have nothing else to think about," said Elvira vaguely. "Look here, Bridget, there's something terribly important I've got to do, and you've got to help me."

"Well, I will if I can. What is it—a man?"

"No, it isn't, as a matter of fact." Bridget looked disappointed. "I've got to get away to Ireland for twenty-four hours or perhaps longer, and you've got to cover up for me."

"To Ireland? Why?"

"I can't tell you all about it now. There's no time. I've got to meet my guardian, Colonel Luscombe, at Prunier's for lunch at half-past one."

"What have you done with the Carpenter?"

"Gave her the slip in Debenham's."

Bridget giggled.

"And after lunch they're taking me down to the Melfords. I'm going to live with them until I'm twenty-one."

"How ghastly!"

"I expect I shall manage. Cousin Mildred is fearfully easy to deceive. It's arranged I'm to come up for classes and things. There's a place called World of Today. They take you to lectures and to museums and to picture galleries and the House of Lords, and all that. The whole point is that nobody will know whether you're where you ought to be or not! We'll manage lots of things."

"I expect we will." Bridget giggled. "We managed in Italy, didn't we? Old Macaroni thought she was so strict. Little did she know what we got up to when we tried."

Both girls laughed in the pleasant consciousness of successful wickedness.

"Still, it did need a lot of planning," said Elvira.

"And some splendid lying," said Bridget. "Have you heard from Guido?"

"Oh yes, he wrote me a long letter signed Ginevra as though he was a girl friend. But I do wish you'd stop talking so much, Bridget. We've got a lot to do and only about an hour and a half to do it in. Now first of all just listen. I'm coming up tomorrow for an appointment with the dentist. That's easy, I can put it off by telephone—or you can from here. Then, about midday, you can ring up the Melfords pretending to be your mother and explain that the dentist wants to see me again the next day and so I'm staying over with you here."

"That ought to go down all right. They'll say how very kind and gush. But supposing you're not back the next day?"

"Then you'll have to do some more ringing up."

Bridget looked doubtful.

"We'll have lots of time to think up something before then," said Elvira impatiently. "What's worrying me now is money. You haven't got any, I suppose?" Elvira spoke without much hope.

"Only about two pounds."

"That's no good. I've got to buy my air ticket. I've looked up the flights. It only takes about two hours. A lot depends upon how long it takes me when I get there."

"Can't you tell me what you're going to do?"

"No, I can't. But it's terribly, terribly important."

Elvira's voice was so different that Bridget looked at her in some surprise.

"Is anything really the matter, Elvira?"

"Yes, it is."

"Is it something nobody's got to know about?"

"Yes, that's the sort of thing. It's frightfully, frightfully secret. I've got to find out if something is really true or not. It's a bore about the money. What's maddening is that I'm really quite rich. My guardian told me so. But all they give me is a measly dress allowance. And that seems to go as soon as I get it."

"Wouldn't your guardian—Colonel Thingummybob —lend you some money?"

"That wouldn't do at all. He'd ask a lot of questions and want to know what I wanted it for."

"Oh dear, I suppose he would. I can't think why everybody wants to ask so many questions. Do you know that if somebody rings me up, Mummy has to ask who it is? When it really is no business of hers!"

Elvira agreed, but her mind was on another tack.

"Have you ever pawned anything, Bridget?"

"Never. I don't think I'd know how to."

"It's quite easy, I believe," said Elvira. "You go to the sort of jeweller who has three balls over the door, isn't that right?"

"I don't think I've got anything that would be any good taking to a pawnbroker," said Bridget.

"Hasn't your mother got some jewellery some- where?"

"I don't think we'd better ask her to help."

"No, perhaps not. But we could pinch something perhaps."

"Oh, I don't think we could do that," said Bridget, shocked.

"No? Well, perhaps you're right. But I bet she wouldn't notice. We could get it back before she missed it. I know. We'll go to Mr. Bollard."

"Who's Mr. Bollard?"

"Oh, he's a sort of family jeweller. I take my watch there always to have it mended. He's known me ever since I was six. Come on, Bridget, we'll go there right away. We'll just have time."

"We'd better go out the back way," said Bridget,

"and then Mummy won't ask us where we're going."

Outside the old established business of Bollard and Whitley in Bond Street the two girls made their final arrangements.

"Are you sure you understand, Bridget?"

"I think so," said Bridget in a far from happy voice.

"First," said Elvira, "we synchronize our watches."

Bridget brightened up a little. This familiar literary phrase had a heartening effect. They solemnly synchronized their watches, Bridget adjusting hers by one minute.

"Zero hour will be twenty-five past exactly," said Elvira. "That will give me plenty of time. Perhaps even more than I need, but it's better that way about."

"But supposing——" began Bridget.

"Supposing what?" asked Elvira.

"Well, I mean, supposing I really got run over?"

"Of course you won't get run over," said Elvira. "You know how nippy you are on your feet, and all London traffic is used to pulling up suddenly. It'll be all right."

Bridget looked far from convinced.

"You won't let me down, Bridget, will you?"

"All right," said Bridget, "I won't let you down."

"Good," said Elvira.

Bridget crossed to the other side of Bond Street and Elvira pushed open the doors of Messrs. Bollard and Whitley, old established jewellers and watchmakers. Inside there was a beautiful and hushed atmosphere. A frock-coated nobleman came forward and asked Elvira what he could do for her.

"Could I see Mr. Bollard?"

"Mr. Bollard. What name shall I say?"

"Miss Elvira Blake."

The nobleman disappeared and Elvira drifted to a

counter where, below plate glass, brooches, rings and bracelets showed off their jewelled proportions against suitable shades of velvet. In a very few moments Mr. Bollard made his appearance. He was the senior partner of the firm, an elderly man of sixty odd. He greeted Elvira with warm friendliness.

"Ah, Miss Blake, so you are in London. It's a great pleasure to see you. Now what can I do for you?"

Elvira produced a dainty little evening wristwatch.

"This watch doesn't go properly," said Elvira. "Could you do something to it?"

"Oh yes, of course. There's no difficulty about that." Mr. Bollard took it from her. "What address shall I send it to?"

Elvira gave the address.

"And there's another thing," she said. "My guardian —Colonel Luscombe you know—"

"Yes, yes, of course."

"He asked me what I'd like for a Christmas present," said Elvira. "He suggested I should come in here and look at some different things. He said would I like him to come with me, and I said I'd rather come along first—because I always think it's rather embarrassing, don't you? I mean, prices and all that."

"Well, that's certainly one aspect," said Mr. Bollard, beaming in an avuncular manner. "Now what had you in mind, Miss Blake? A brooch, bracelet—a ring?"

"I think really brooches are most useful," said Elvira. "But I wonder—could I look at a lot of things?" She looked up at him appealing. He smiled sympathetically.

"Of course, of course. No pleasure at all if one has to make up one's mind too quickly, is it?"

The next five or six minutes were spent very agreeably. Nothing was too much trouble for Mr. Bollard.

He fetched things from one case and another, brooches and bracelets piled up on the piece of velvet spread in front of Elvira. Occasionally she turned aside to look at herself in a mirror, trying the effect of a brooch or a pendant. Finally, rather uncertainly, a pretty little bangle, a small diamond wristwatch and two brooches were laid aside.

"We'll make a note of these," said Mr. Bollard, "and then when Colonel Luscombe is in London next, perhaps he'll come in and see what he decides he'd like to give you."

"I think that way will be very nice," said Elvira. "Then he'll feel more that he's chosen my present himself, won't he?" Her limpid blue gaze was raised to the jeweller's face. That same blue gaze had registered a moment earlier that the time was now exactly twenty-five minutes past the hour.

Outside there was the squealing of brakes and a girl's loud scream. Inevitably the eyes of everyone in the shop turned towards the windows of the shop giving on Bond Street. The movement of Elvira's hand on the counter in front of her and then to the pocket of her neat tailor-made coat and skirt was so rapid and unobtrusive as to be almost unnoticeable, even if anybody had been looking.

"Tcha, tcha," said Mr. Bollard, turning back from where he had been peering out into the street. "Very nearly an accident. Silly girl! Rushing across the road like that."

Elvira was already moving towards the door. She looked at her wristwatch and uttered an exclamation.

"Oh dear, I've been far too long in here. I shall miss my train back to the country. Thank you so much, Mr. Bollard, and you won't forget which the four things are, will you?"

In another minute she was out of the door. Turning rapidly to the left and then to the left again, she stopped in the arcade of a shoe shop until Bridget, rather breathless, rejoined her.

"Oh," said Bridget, "I was terrified. I thought I was going to be killed. And I've torn a hole in my stocking, too."

"Never mind," said Elvira and walked her friend rapidly along the street and round yet another corner to the right. "Come on."

"Is it—was it—all right?"

Elvira's hand slipped into her pocket and out again showing the diamond and sapphire bracelet in her palm.

"Oh, Elvira, how you dared!"

"Now, Bridget, you've got to get along to the pawn-shop we marked down. Go in and see how much you can get for this. Ask for a hundred."

"Do you think—supposing they say—I mean—I mean, it might be on a list of stolen things—"

"Don't be silly. How could it be on a list so soon? They haven't even noticed it's gone yet."

"But Elvira, when they do notice it's gone, they'll think—perhaps they'll know—that you must have taken it."

"They might think so—if they discover it soon."

"Well, then they'll go to the police and—"

She stopped as Elvira shook her head slowly, her pale yellow hair swinging to and fro and a faint enigmatic smile curving up the corners of her mouth.

"They won't go to the police, Bridget. Certainly not if they think I took it."

"Why—you mean—?"

"As I told you, I'm going to have a lot of money when I'm twenty-one. I shall be able to buy lots of

71

jewels from them. They won't make a scandal. Go on and get the money quick. Then go to Aer Lingus and book the ticket—I must take a taxi to Prunier's. I'm already ten minutes late. I'll be with you tomorrow morning by half-past ten."

"Oh Elvira, I wish you wouldn't take such frightful risks," moaned Bridget.

But Elvira had hailed a taxi.

II

Miss Marple had a very enjoyable time at Robinson and Cleaver's. Besides purchasing expensive but delicious sheets—she loved linen sheets with their texture and their coolness—she also indulged in a purchase of good quality red-bordered dish cloths. Really the difficulty in getting proper dish cloths nowadays! Instead, you were offered things that might as well have been ornamental tablecloths, decorated with radishes or lobsters on the Tour Eiffel or Trafalgar Square, or else littered with lemons and oranges. Having given her address in St. Mary Mead, Miss Marple found a convenient bus which took her to the Army and Navy Stores.

The Army and Navy Stores had been a haunt of Miss Marple's aunt in days long gone. It was not, of course, quite the same nowadays. Miss Marple cast her thoughts back to Aunt Helen seeking out her own special man in the grocery department, settling herself comfortably in a chair, wearing a bonnet and what she always called her "black poplin" mantle. Then there would ensue a long hour with nobody in a hurry and Aunt Helen thinking of every conceivable grocery that could be purchased and stored up for future use. Christmas was provided for, and there was even a far-off look towards Easter. The young Jane had fidgeted somewhat, and had been told to go and look at the glass department by way of amusement.

Having finished her purchases, Aunt Helen would then proceed to lengthy inquiries about her chosen shop-assistant's mother, wife, second boy, and crippled sister-in-law. Having had a thoroughly pleasant morning, Aunt Helen would say in the playful manner of those times "And how would a little girl feel about some luncheon?" Whereupon they went up in the lift to the fourth floor and had luncheon, which always finished with a strawberry ice. After that, they bought half a pound of coffee chocolate creams and went to a matinee in a four-wheeler.

Of course, the Army and Navy Stores had had a good many face lifts since those days. In fact, it was now quite unrecognizable from the old days. It was gayer and much brighter. Miss Marple, though throwing a kindly and indulgent smile at the past, did not object to the amenities of the present. There was still a restaurant, and there she repaired to order her lunch.

As she was looking carefully down the menu and deciding what to have, she looked across the room and her eyebrows went up a little. How extraordinary coincidence was! Here was a woman she had never seen till the day before, though she had seen plenty of newspaper photographs of her—at race meetings, in Bermuda, or standing by her own plane or car. Yesterday, for the first time, she had seen her in the flesh. And now, as was so often the case, there was the coincidence of running into her again in a most unlikely place. For somehow she did not connect lunch at the Army and Navy Stores with Bess Sedgwick. She would not have been surprised to see Bess Sedg-

wick emerging from a den in Soho, or stepping out of
Covent Garden Opera House in evening dress with a
diamond tiara on her head. But somehow, not in the
Army and Navy Stores which in Miss Marple's mind
was, and always would be, connected with the armed
forces, their wives, daughters, aunts and grandmothers.
Still, there Bess Sedgwick was, looking as usual very
smart, in her dark suit and her emerald shirt, lunching
at a table with a man. A young man with a lean
hawklike face, wearing a black leather jacket. They
were leaning forward talking earnestly together, fork-
ing mouthfuls of food as though they were quite un-
aware what they were eating.

An assignation, perhaps? Yes, probably an assignation. The man must be fifteen or twenty years younger
than she was—but Bess Sedgwick was a magnetically
attractive woman.

Miss Marple looked at the young man consideringly
and decided that he was what she called a "handsome
fellow." She also decided that she didn't like him very
much. "Just like Harry Russell," said Miss Marple to
herself, dredging up a prototype as usual from the past.
"Never up to any good. Never did any woman who
had anything to do with him any good either."

She wouldn't take advice from me, thought Miss
Marple, but I could give her some. However, other
people's love affairs were no concern of hers, and
Bess Sedgwick, by all accounts, could take care of
herself very well when it came to love affairs.

Miss Marple sighed, ate her lunch, and meditated a
visit to the stationery department.

Curiosity, or what she preferred herself to call
"taking an interest" in other people's affairs was un-
doubtedly one of Miss Marple's characteristics.

Deliberately leaving her gloves on the table, she rose and crossed the floor to the cash desk, taking a route that passed close to Lady Sedgwick's table. Having paid her bill she "discovered" the absence of her gloves and returned to get them—unfortunately dropping her handbag on the return route. It came open and spilled various oddments. A waitress rushed to assist her in picking them up, and Miss Marple was forced to show a great shakiness and dropped coins and keys a second time.

She did not get very much by these subterfuges but they were not entirely in vain—and it was interesting that neither of the two objects of her curiosity spared as much as a glance for the dithery old lady who kept dropping things.

As Miss Marple waited for the elevator down she memorized such scraps as she had heard.

"What about the weather forecast?"

"O.K. No fog."

"All set for Lucerne?"

"Yes. Plane leaves 9.40."

That was all she had got the first time. On the way back it had lasted a little longer.

Bess Sedgwick had been speaking angrily.

"What possessed you to come to Bertram's yesterday—you shouldn't have come near the place."

"It's all right. I asked if you were staying there and everyone knows we're close friends—"

"That's not the point. Bertram's is all right for me —not for you. You stick out like a sore thumb. Everyone stares at you."

"Let them!"

"You really are an idiot. Why—why? What reasons did you have? You *had* a reason—I know you. . . ."

"Calm down, Bess."

"You're such a liar!"

That was all Miss Marple had been able to hear. She found it interesting.

7

On the evening of November 19 Canon Pennyfather
had finished an early dinner at the Athenaeum, he had
nodded to one or two friends, had had a pleasant acri-
monious discussion on some crucial points of the dat-
ing of the Dead Sea scrolls and now, glancing at his
watch, saw that it was time to leave to catch his
plane to Lucerne. As he passed through the hall he
was greeted by one more friend: Dr. Whittaker, of the
S.O.A.S., who said cheerfully, "How are you, Pennyfather? Haven't seen you for a long time. How did you
get on at the Congress? Any points of interest come
up?"

"I am sure there will be."

"Just come back from it, haven't you?"

"No, no, I am on my way there. I'm catching a
plane this evening."

"Oh I see." Whittaker looked slightly puzzled.
"Somehow or other I thought the Congress was today."

"No, no. Tomorrow, the nineteenth."

Canon Pennyfather passed out through the door
while his friend, looking after him, was just saying,

"But my dear chap, today is the nineteenth, isn't it?"

Canon Pennyfather, however, was gone beyond earshot. He picked up a taxi in Pall Mall, and was driven to the air terminal in Kensington. There was quite a fair crowd this evening. Presenting himself at the desk it at last came to his turn. He managed to produce ticket and passport and other necessities for the journey. The girl behind the desk, about to stamp these credentials, paused abruptly.

"I beg your pardon, sir, this seems to be the wrong ticket."

"The wrong ticket? No, no, that is quite right. Flight one hundred and—well, I can't really read without my glasses—one hundred and something to Lucerne."

"It's the date, sir. This is dated Wednesday the eighteenth."

"No, no, surely. At least—I mean—today is Wednesday the eighteenth."

"I'm sorry, sir. Today is the nineteenth."

"The nineteenth!" The Canon was dismayed. He fished out a small diary, turning the pages eagerly. In the end he had to be convinced. Today was the nineteenth. The plane he had meant to catch had gone yesterday.

"Then that means—that means—dear me, it means the Congress at Lucerne has taken place today."

He stared in deep dismay across the counter; but there were many others travelling; the canon and his perplexities were elbowed aside. He stood sadly, holding the useless ticket in his hand. His mind ranged over various possibilities. Perhaps his ticket could be changed? But that would be no use—no indeed—what time was it now? Going on for nine o'clock? The conference had actually taken place; starting at ten o'clock this morning. Of course, that was what Whittaker had meant at the Athenaeum. He thought Canon Pennyfather had already been to the Congress.

"Oh dear, oh dear," said Canon Pennyfather, to himself. "What a muddle I have made of it all!" He wandered sadly and silently into the Cromwell Road, not at its best a very cheerful place.

He walked slowly along the street carrying his bag and revolving perplexities in his mind. When at last he had worked out to his satisfaction the various reasons for which he had made a mistake in the day, he shook his head sadly.

"Now, I suppose," he said to himself, "I suppose— let me see, it's after nine o'clock, yes, I suppose I had better have something to eat."

It was curious, he thought, that he did not feel hungry.

Wandering disconsolately along the Cromwell Road he finally settled upon a small restaurant which served Indian curries. It seemed to him that though he was not quite as hungry as he ought to be, he had better keep his spirits up by having a meal, and after that he must find a hotel and—but no, there was no need to do that. He had a hotel! Of course. He was staying at Bertram's, and had reserved his room for four days. What a piece of luck! What a splendid piece of luck! So his room was there, waiting for him. He had only to ask for his key at the desk and—here another reminiscence assailed him. Something heavy in his pocket?

He dipped his hand in and brought out one of those large and solid keys with which hotels try and discourage their vaguer guests from taking them away in their pockets. It had not prevented the canon from doing so!

"Number Nineteen," said the canon, in happy recognition. "That's right. It's very fortunate that I haven't got to go and find a room in a hotel. They say they're very crowded just now. Yes, Edmunds was saying so at the Athenaeum this evening. He had a terrible job finding a room."

Somewhat pleased with himself and the care he had taken over his travelling arrangements by booking a hotel beforehand, the canon abandoned his curry, remembered to pay for it, and strode out once more into the Cromwell Road.

It seemed a little tame to go home just like this when he ought to have been dining in Lucerne and talking about all sorts of interesting and fascinating problems. His eye was caught by a movie theater sign: *Walls of Jericho*. It seemed an eminently suitable title. It would be interesting to see if Biblical accuracy had been preserved.

He bought himself a seat and stumbled into the darkness. He enjoyed the film, though it seemed to him to have no relationship to the Biblical story whatsoever. Even Joshua seemed to have been left out. The walls of Jericho seemed to be a symbolical way of referring to a certain lady's marriage vows. When they had tumbled down several times, the beautiful star met the dour and uncouth hero whom she had secretly loved all along and between them they proposed to build up the walls in a way that would stand the test of time better. It was not a film destined particularly to appeal to an elderly clergyman; but Canon Pennyfather enjoyed it very much. It was not the sort of film he often saw and he felt it was enlarging his knowledge of life. The film ended, the lights went up, the national anthem was played and Canon Pennyfather stumbled out into the lights of London, slightly consoled for the sad events earlier in the evening.

It was a fine night and he walked home to Bertram's Hotel after first getting into a bus which took him in the opposite direction. It was midnight when he got in, and Bertram's Hotel at midnight usually preserved a decorous appearance of everyone having gone to bed. The elevator was on a higher floor so the canon walked up the stairs. He came to his room, inserted the key in the lock, threw the door open and entered!

Good gracious, was he seeing things? But who—how —he saw the upraised arm too late. . . .

Stars exploded in a kind of Guy Fawkes display within his head. . . .

8

The Irish Mail rushed through the night. Or, more correctly, through the darkness of the early morning hours.

At intervals the diesel engine gave its weird banshee warning cry. It was travelling at well over eighty miles an hour. It was on time.

Then, with some suddenness, the pace slackened as the brakes came on. The wheels screamed as they gripped the metals. Slower . . . slower. . . . The guard put his head out of the window, noting the red signal ahead as the train came to a final halt. Some of the passengers woke up. Most did not.

One elderly lady, alarmed by the suddenness of the deceleration, opened up the door and looked out along the corridor. A little way along one of the doors to the line was open. An elderly cleric with a thatch of thick white hair was climbing up from the permanent way. She presumed he had previously climbed down to the line to investigate.

The morning air was distinctly chilly. Someone at the end of the corridor said, "Only a signal." The elderly lady withdrew into her compartment and tried to go to sleep again.

Farther up the line, a man waving a lantern was running towards the train from a signal box. The fireman climbed down from the engine. The guard who had descended from the train came along to join him. The man with the lantern arrived, rather short of breath and spoke in a series of gasps.

"Bad crash ahead . . . freight train derailed. . . ."

The engine driver looked out of his cab, then climbed down also to join the others.

At the rear of the train, six men who had just climbed up the embankment boarded the train through a door left open for them in the last coach. Six passengers from different coaches met them. With well rehearsed speed, they proceeded to take charge of the mail car, isolating it from the rest of the train. Two men in Balaclava helmets at front and rear of the compartment stood on guard, coshes in hand.

A man in railway uniform went forward along the corridor of the stationary train, uttering explanations to such as demanded them.

"Block on the line ahead. Ten minutes' delay, maybe, not much more. . . ." It sounded friendly and reassuring.

By the engine, the driver and the fireman lay neatly gagged and trussed up. The man with the lantern called out: "Everything O.K. here."

The guard lay by the embankment, similarly gagged and tied.

The expert cracksmen in the mail car had done their work. Two more neatly trussed bodies lay on the floor. The special mailbags sailed out to where other men on the embankment awaited them.

In their compartments, passengers grumbled to each other that the railways were not what they used to be.

Then, as they settled themselves to sleep again, there

came through the darkness the roar of an exhaust.

"Goodness," murmured a woman. "Is that a jet plane?"

"Racing car, I should say."

The roar died away. . . .

On the Bedhampton Motorway, nine miles away, a steady stream of night lorries was grinding its way north. A big white racing car flashed past them.

Ten minutes later, it turned off the motorway.

The garage on the corner of the B road bore the sign CLOSED. But the big doors swung open and the white car was driven straight in, the doors closing again behind it. Three men worked at lightning speed. A fresh set of license plates were attached. The driver changed his coat and cap. He had worn white sheepskin before. Now he wore black leather. He drove out again. Three minutes after his departure, an old Morris Oxford, driven by a clergyman, chugged out on to the road and proceeded to take a route through various turning and twisting country lanes.

A station wagon, driven along a country road slowed up as it came upon an old Morris Oxford, parked by a hedge, with an elderly man standing over it.

The driver of the station wagon put out a head. "Having trouble? Can I help?"

"Very good of you. It's my lights."

The two drivers approached each other—listened. "All clear."

Various expensive American-style suitcases were transferred from the Morris Oxford to the station wagon.

A mile or two farther on, the station wagon turned off on what looked like a rough track but which presently turned out to be the back way to a large and opulent mansion. In what had been a stableyard, a big white Mercedes car was standing. The driver of the station wagon opened its trunk with a key, transferred the cases to the trunk, and drove away again in the station wagon.

In a nearby farmyard a cock crowed noisily.

9

Elvira Blake looked up at the sky, noted that it was a fine morning and went into a telephone box. She dialled Bridget's number in Onslow Square. Satisfied by the response, she said, "Hello? Bridget?"

"Oh, Elvira, is that you?" Bridget's voice sounded agitated.

"Yes. Has everything been all right?"

"Oh no. It's been *awful*. Your cousin, Mrs. Melford, rang up Mummy yesterday afternoon."

"What, about me?"

"Yes. I thought I'd done it so well when I rang her up at lunchtime. But it seems she got worried about your teeth. Thought there might be something really wrong with them. Abscesses or something. So she rang up the dentist herself and found, of course, that you'd never been there at all. So then she rang up Mummy and unfortunately Mummy was right there by the telephone. So I couldn't get there first. And naturally Mummy said she didn't know anything about it, and that you certainly weren't staying here. I didn't know what to do."

"What did you do?"

"Pretended I knew nothing about it. I did say I

86

thought you'd said something about going to see some friends at Wimbledon."

"Why Wimbledon?"

"It was the first place came into my head."

Elvira sighed. "Oh well, I suppose I'll have to cook up something. An old governess, perhaps, who lives at Wimbledon. All this fussing does makes things so complicated. I hope Cousin Mildred doesn't make a real fool of herself and ring up the police or something like that?"

"Are you going down there now?"

"Not till this evening. I've got a lot to do first."

"You got to Ireland. Was it—all right?"

"I found out what I wanted to know."

"You sound—sort of grim."

"I'm feeling grim."

"Can't I help you, Elvira? Do anything?"

"Nobody can help me really. . . . It's a thing I have to do myself. I hoped something wasn't true, but it is true. I don't know quite what to do about it."

"Are you in danger, Elvira?"

"Don't be melodramatic, Bridget. I'll have to be careful that's all. I'll have to be very careful."

"Then you are in danger."

Elvira said after a moment's pause, "I expect I'm just imagining things, that's all."

"Elvira, what are you going to do about that bracelet?"

"Oh, that's all right. I've arranged to get some money from someone, so I can go and—what's the word?—redeem it. Then just take it back to Bollards."

"D'you think they'll be all right about it? . . . No, Mummy, it's just the laundry. They say we never sent that sheet. Yes, Mummy, yes, I'll tell the manageress. All right then."

At the other end of the line Elvira grinned and put down the receiver. She opened her purse, sorted through her money, counted out the coins she needed and arranged them in front of her and proceeded to put through a call. When she got the number she wanted she put in the necessary coins, pressed Button A and spoke in a small rather breathless voice.

"Hello, Cousin Mildred. Yes, it's me . . . I'm terribly sorry. . . . Yes, I know . . . well I was going to . . . yes it was dear old Maddy, you know our old Mademoiselle. . . . Yes, I wrote a postcard, then I forgot to post it. It's still in my pocket now. . . . Well, you see she was ill and there was no one to look after her and so I just stopped to see she was all right. Yes, I was going to Bridget's but this changed things . . . I don't understand about the message you got. Someone must have jumbled it up. . . . Yes, I'll explain it all to you when I get back. . . . yes, this afternoon. No, I shall just wait and see the nurse who's coming to look after old Maddy—well, not really a nurse. You know one of those—er—practical aid nurses or something like that. No, she would hate to go to hospital. . . . But I am sorry, Cousin Mildred, I really am very, very sorry." She put down the receiver and sighed in an exasperated manner. "If only," she murmured to herself, "one didn't have to tell so many lies to everybody."

She came out of the telephone box, noting as she did so the big newspaper placards: BIG TRAIN ROBBERY. IRISH MAIL ATTACKED BY BANDITS

II

Mr. Bollard was serving a customer when the shop door opened. He looked up to see the Honourable Elvira Blake entering.

"No," she said to an assistant who came forward to her. "I'd rather wait until Mr. Bollard is free."

Presently Mr. Bollard's customer's business was concluded and Elvira moved into the vacant place.

"Good morning, Mr. Bollard," she said.

"I'm afraid your watch isn't done quite as soon as this, Miss Elvira," said Mr. Bollard.

"Oh, it's not the watch," said Elvira. "I've come to apologize. A dreadful thing happened." She opened her bag and took out a small box. From it she extracted the sapphire and diamond bracelet. "You will remember when I came in with my watch to be repaired that I was looking at things for a Christmas present and there was an accident outside in the street. Somebody was run over I think, or nearly run over. I suppose I must have had the bracelet in my hand and put it into the pocket of my suit without thinking, although I only found it this morning. So I rushed along at once to bring it back. I'm so terribly sorry, Mr. Bollard, I don't know how I came to do such an idiotic thing."

"Why, that's quite all right, Miss Elvira," said Mr. Bollard slowly.

"I suppose you thought someone had stolen it," said Elvira.

Her limpid blue eyes met his.

"We had discovered its loss," said Mr. Bollard. "Thank you very much, Miss Elvira, for bringing it back so promptly."

"I felt simply awful about it when I found it," said Elvira. "Well, thank you very much, Mr. Bollard, for being so nice about it."

"A lot of strange mistakes do occur," said Mr. Bollard. He smiled at her in an avuncular manner. "We won't think of it any more. But don't do it again, though." He laughed with the air of one making a genial little joke.

"Oh no," said Elvira, "I shall be terribly careful in future."

She smiled at him, turned and left the shop.

"Now I wonder," said Mr. Bollard to himself, "I really do wonder. . . ."

One of his partners, who had been standing near, moved nearer to him. "So she did take it," he said.

"Yes. She took it all right," said Mr. Bollard.

"But she brought it back," his partner pointed out.

"She brought it back," agreed Mr. Bollard. "I didn't actually expect that."

"You mean you didn't expect her to bring it back?"

"No, not if it was she who'd taken it."

"Do you think her story is true?" his partner inquired curiously. "I mean, that she slipped it into her pocket by accident?"

"I suppose it's possible," said Bollard thoughtfully.

"Or it could be kleptomania, I suppose."

"Or it could be kleptomania," agreed Bollard. "It's more likely that she took it on purpose. . . . But if so, why did she bring it back so soon? It's curious—"

"Just as well we didn't notify the police. I admit I wanted to."

"I know, I know. You haven't got as much experience as I have. In this case, it was definitely better not." He added softly to himself, "The thing's interesting, though. Quite interesting. I wonder how old she is? Seventeen or eighteen, I suppose. She might have got herself in a jam of some kind."

"I thought you said she was rolling in money."

"You may be an heiress and rolling in money," said Bollard, "but at seventeen you can't always get your hands on it. The funny thing is, you know, they keep heiresses much shorter of cash than they keep the more impecunious. It's not always a good idea. Well, I don't suppose we shall ever know the truth of it."

He put the bracelet back in its place in the display case and shut down the lid.

10

The offices of Egerton, Forbes and Wilborough were in Bloomsbury, in one of those imposing and dignified squares which have as yet not felt the wind of change. Their brass plate was suitably worn down to illegibility. The firm had been going for over a hundred years and a good proportion of the landed gentry of England were their clients. There was no Forbes in the firm any more and no Wilboroughs. Instead there were Atkinsons, father and son, and a Welsh Lloyd and a Scottish MacAllister. There was, however, still an Egerton, descendant of the original Egerton. This particular Egerton was a man of fifty-two and he was adviser to several families which had in their day been advised by his grandfather, his uncle, and his father.

At this moment he was sitting behind a large mahogany desk in his handsome room on the first floor, speaking kindly but firmly to a dejected-looking client. Richard Egerton was a handsome man, tall, dark with a touch of grey at the temples and very shrewd grey eyes. His advice was always good advice, but he seldom minced his words.

"Quite frankly you haven't got a leg to stand upon,

Freddie," he was saying. "Not with those letters you've written."

"You don't think—" Freddie murmured dejectedly.

"No, I don't," said Egerton. "The only hope is to settle out of court. It might even be held that you've rendered yourself liable to criminal prosecution."

"Oh, look here, Richard, that's carrying things a bit far."

There was a small discreet buzz on Egerton's desk. He picked up the telephone receiver with a frown.

"I thought I said I wasn't to be disturbed."

There was a murmur at the other end. Egerton said, "Oh. Yes—yes, I see. Ask her to wait, will you."

He replaced the receiver and turned once more to his unhappy-looking client.

"Look here, Freddie," he said, "I know the law and you don't. You're in a nasty jam. I'll do my best to get you out of it, but it's going to cost you a bit. I doubt if they'd settle for less than twelve thousand."

"Twelve thousand!" The unfortunate Freddie was aghast. "Oh, I say! I haven't got it, Richard."

"Well, you'll have to raise it then. There are always ways and means. If she'll settle for twelve thousand, you'll be lucky, and if you fight the case, it'll cost you a lot more."

"You lawyers!" said Freddie. "Sharks, all of you!"

He rose to his feet. "Well," he said, "do your bloody best for me, Richard old boy."

He took his departure, shaking his head sadly. Richard Egerton put Freddie and his affairs out of his mind, and thought about his next client. He said softly to himself, "The Honourable Elvira Blake. I wonder what she's like. . . ." He lifted his receiver. "Lord Frederick's gone. Send up Miss Blake, will you."

As he waited he made little calculations on his desk

pad. How many years since——? She must be fifteen—
seventeen—perhaps even more than that. Time went
so fast. Coniston's daughter, he thought, and Bess's
daughter. I wonder which of them she takes after?

The door opened, the clerk announced Miss Elvira
Blake and the girl walked into the room. Egerton rose
from his chair and came towards her. In appearance,
he thought, she did not resemble either of her parents.
Tall, slim, very fair, Bess's colouring but none of
Bess's vitality, with an old-fashioned air about her;
though that was difficult to be sure of, since the
fashion in dress happened at the moment to be ruffles
and baby bodices.

"Well, well," he said, as he shook hands with her.
"This is a surprise. Last time I saw you, you were
eleven years old. Come and sit here." He pulled forward a chair and she sat down.

"I suppose," said Elvira, a little uncertainly, "that I
ought to have written first. Written and made an appointment. Something like that, but I really made up
my mind very suddenly and it seemed an opportunity,
since I was in London."

"And what are you doing in London?"

"Having my teeth seen to."

"Beastly things, teeth," said Egerton. "Give us
trouble from the cradle to the grave. But I am grateful
for the teeth, if it gives me an opportunity of seeing
you. Let me see now; you've been in Italy, haven't
you, finished your education there at one of these
places all girls go to nowadays?"

"Yes," said Elvira, "the Contessa Martinelli. But I've
left there now for good. I'm living with the Melfords
in Kent until I make up my mind if there's anything
I'd like to do."

"Well, I hope you'll find something satisfactory.

You're not thinking of a university or anything like that?"

"No," said Elvira, "I don't think I'd be clever enough for that." She paused before saying, "I suppose you'd have to agree to anything if I did want to do it?"

Egerton's keen eyes focused sharply.

"I am one of your guardians, and a trustee under your father's will, yes," he said. "Therefore, you have a perfect right to approach me at any time."

Elvira said "Thank you," politely.

"Is there anything worrying you?" Egerton asked.

"No. Not really. But you see, I don't know anything. Nobody's ever told me things. One doesn't always like to ask."

He looked at her attentively.

"You mean things about yourself?"

"Yes," said Elvira. "It's kind of you to understand. Uncle Derek—" she hesitated.

"Derek Luscombe, you mean?"

"Yes. I've always called him uncle."

"I see."

"He's very kind," said Elvira, "but he's not the sort of person who ever tells you anything. He just arranges things, and looks a little worried in case they mightn't be what I'd like. Of course he listens to a lot of people —women, I mean—who tell him things. Like Contessa Martinelli. He arranges for me to go to schools or to finishing places."

"And they haven't been where you wanted to go?"

"No, I didn't mean that. They've been quite all right. I mean they've been more or less where everyone else goes."

"I see."

"But I don't know anything about myself. I mean

95

what money I've got, and how much, and what I could do with it if I wanted."

"In fact," said Egerton, with his attractive smile, "you want to talk business. Is that it? Well, I think you're quite right. Let's see. How old are you? Sixteen —seventeen?"

"I'm nearly twenty."

"Oh dear. I'd no idea."

"You see," explained Elvira, "I feel all the time that I'm being shielded and sheltered. It's nice in a way, but it can get very irritating."

"It's an attitude that's gone out of date," agreed Egerton, "but I can quite see that it would appeal to Derek Luscombe."

"He's a dear," said Elvira, "but very difficult, somehow, to talk to seriously."

"Yes, I can see that that might be so. Well, how much do you know about yourself, Elvira? About your family circumstances?"

"I know that my father died when I was five and that my mother had run away from him with someone when I was about two, I don't remember her at all. I barely remember my father. He was very old and had his leg up on a chair. He used to swear. I was rather scared of him. After he died I lived first with an aunt or a cousin or something of my father's, until she died, and then I lived with Uncle Derek and his sister. But then she died and I went to Italy. Uncle Derek has arranged for me, now, to live with the Melfords who are his cousins and very kind and nice and have two daughters about my age."

"You're happy there?"

"I don't know yet. I've barely got there. They're all very dull. I really wanted to know how much money I've got."

"So it's financial information you really want?"

"Yes," said Elvira. "I've got some money, I know. Is it a lot?"

Egerton was serious now. "Yes," he said. "You've got a lot of money. Your father was a very rich man. You were his only child. When he died, the title and the estate went to a cousin. He didn't like the cousin, so he left all his personal property, which was considerable, to his daughter—to you, Elvira. You're a very rich woman, or will be, when you are twenty-one."

"You mean I am not rich now?"

"Yes," said Egerton, "you're rich now, but the money is not yours to dispose of until you are twenty-one or marry. Until that time it is in the hands of your trustees. Luscombe, myself and another." He smiled at her. "We haven't embezzled it or anything like that. It's still there. In fact, we've increased your capital considerably by investments."

"How much will I have?"

"At the age of twenty-one or upon your marriage, you will come into a sum which at a rough estimate would amount to six or seven hundred thousand pounds."

"That is a lot," said Elvira, impressed.

"Yes, it is a lot. Probably it is because it is such a lot that nobody has ever talked to you about it much."

He watched her as she reflected upon this. Quite an interesting girl, he thought. Looked an unbelievably milk-and-water miss, but she was more than that. A good deal more. He said, with a faintly ironic smile, "Does that satisfy you?"

She gave him a sudden smile.

"It ought to, oughtn't it?"

"Rather better than winning the pools," he suggested.

She nodded, but her mind was elsewhere. Then she came out abruptly with a question.

"Who gets it if I die?"

"As things stand now, it would go to your next of kin."

"I mean—I couldn't make a will now, could I? Not until I was twenty-one. That's what someone told me."

"They were quite right."

"That's really rather annoying. If I was married and died, I suppose my husband would get the money?"

"Yes."

"And if I wasn't married, my mother would be my next of kin and get it. I really seem to have very few relations—I don't even know my mother. What is she like?"

"She's a very remarkable woman," said Egerton shortly. "Everybody would agree to that."

"Didn't she ever want to see me?"

"She may have done . . . I think it's very possible that she did. But having made in—certain ways—rather a mess of her own life, she may have thought that it was better for you that you should be brought up quite apart from her."

"Do you actually know that she thinks that?"

"No. I don't really know anything about it."

Elvira got up. "Thank you," she said. "It's very kind of you to tell me all this."

"I think perhaps you ought to have been told more about things before," said Egerton.

"It's rather humiliating not to know things," said Elvira. "Uncle Derek, of course, thinks I'm just a child."

"Well, he's not a very young man himself. He and I,

you know, are well advanced in years. You must make allowances for us when we look at things from the point of view of our advanced age."

Elvira stood looking at him for a moment or two. "But you don't think I'm really a child, do you?" she said shrewdly, and added, "I expect you know rather more about girls than Uncle Derek does. He just lived with his sister." Then she stretched out her hand and said, very prettily, "Thank you so much. I hope I haven't interrupted some important work you had to do," and went out.

Egerton stood looking at the door that had closed behind her. He pursed up his lips, whistled a moment, shook his head and sat down again, picked up a pen and tapped thoughtfully on his desk. He drew some papers towards him, then thrust them back and picked up his telephone.

"Miss Cordell, get me Colonel Luscombe, will you? Try his club first. And then the Shropshire address."

He put back the receiver. Again he drew his papers towards him and started reading them but his mind was not on what he was doing. Presently his buzzer went.

"Colonel Luscombe is on the wire now, Mr. Egerton."

"Right. Put him through. Hello, Derek. Richard Egerton here. How are you? I've just been having a visit from someone you know. A visit from your ward."

"From Elvira?" Derek Luscombe sounded very surprised.

"Yes."

"But why—what on earth—what did she come to you for? Not in any trouble?"

"No, I wouldn't say so. On the contrary, she seemed

rather—well, pleased with herself. She wanted to know all about her financial position."

"You didn't tell her, I hope?" said Colonel Luscombe, in alarm.

"Why not? What's the point of secrecy?"

"Well, I can't help feeling it's a little unwise for a girl to know that she is going to come into such a large amount of money."

"Somebody else will tell her that, if we don't. She's got to be prepared, you know. Money is a responsibility."

"Yes, but she's so much of a child still."

"Are you sure of that?"

"What do you mean? Of course she's a child."

"I wouldn't describe her as such. Who's the boy friend?"

"I beg your pardon."

"I said who's the boy friend? There *is* a boy friend in the offing, isn't there?"

"No, indeed. Nothing of the sort. What on earth makes you think that?"

"Nothing that she actually said. But I've got some experience, you know. I think you'll find there is a boy friend."

"Well, I can assure you you're quite wrong. I mean, she's been most carefully brought up, she's been at very strict schools; she's been in a very select finishing establishment in Italy. I should know if there was anything of that kind going on. I dare say she's met one or two pleasant young fellows and all that, but I'm sure there's nothing of the kind you suggest."

"Well, my diagnosis is a boy friend—and probably an undesirable one."

"But why, Richard, why? What do you know about young girls?"

"Quite a lot," said Egerton dryly. "I've had three clients in the last year, two of whom were made wards of court and the third one managed to bully her parents into agreeing to an almost certainly disastrous marriage. Girls don't get looked after the way they used to be. Conditions are such that it's very difficult to look after them at all—"

"But I assure you Elvira has been most carefully looked after."

"The ingenuity of the young female of the species is beyond anything you could conjecture! You keep an eye on her, Derek. Make a few inquiries as to what she's been up to."

"Nonsense. She's just a sweet simple girl."

"What you don't know about sweet simple girls would fill an album! Her mother ran away and caused a scandal—remember?—when she was younger than Elvira is today. As for old Coniston, he was one of the worst rips in England."

"You upset me, Richard. You upset me very much."

"You might as well be warned. What I didn't quite like was one of her other questions. Why is she so anxious to know who'd inherit her money if she dies?"

"It's queer your saying that, because she asked me that same question."

"Did she now? Why should her mind run on early death? She asked me about her mother, by the way."

Colonel Luscombe's voice sounded worried as he said, "I wish Bess would get in touch with the girl."

"Have you been talking to her on the subject—to Bess, I mean?"

"Well, yes. . . . Yes I did. I ran across her by chance. We were staying in the same hotel, as a matter of fact. I urged Bess to make some arrangements to see the girl."

"What did she say?" asked Egerton curiously.

"Refused point blank. She more or less said that she wasn't a safe person for the girl to know."

"Looked at from one point of view I don't suppose she is," said Egerton. "She's mixed up with that racing fellow, isn't she?"

"I've heard rumours."

"Yes, I've heard them too. I don't know if there's much in it really. There might be, I suppose. That could be why she feels as she does. Bess's friends are strong meat from time to time! But what a woman she is, eh, Derek? What a woman."

"Always been her own worst enemy," said Derek Luscombe gruffly.

"A really nice conventional remark," said Egerton. "Well, sorry I bothered you, Derek, but keep a look out for undersirables in the background. Don't say you haven't been warned."

He replaced the receiver and drew the pages on his desk towards him once more. This time he was able to put his whole attention on what he was doing.

11

Mrs. McCrea, Canon Pennyfather's housekeeper, had ordered a Dover sole for the evening of his return. The advantages attached to a good Dover sole were manifold. It need not be introduced to the grill or frying pan until the canon was safely in the house. It could be kept until the next day if necessary. Canon Pennyfather was fond of Dover sole; and, if a telephone call or telegram arrived saying that the canon would after all be elsewhere on this particular evening, Mrs. McCrae was fond of a good Dover sole herself. All therefore was in good trim for the canon's return. The Dover sole would be followed by pancakes. The sole sat on the kitchen table, the batter for the pancakes was ready in a bowl. All was in readiness. The brass shone, the silver sparkled, not a minuscule of dust showed anywhere. There was only one thing lacking. The canon himself.

The canon was scheduled to return on the train arriving at six-thirty from London.

At seven o'clock he had not returned. No doubt the train was late. At seven-thirty he still had not returned. Mrs. McCrae gave a sigh of vexation. She suspected that this was going to be another of these things. Eight o'clock came and no canon. Mrs. McCrae gave a long, exasperated sigh. Soon, no doubt, she would get a telephone call, though it was quite within the bounds of possibility that there would not even be a telephone call. He might have written to her. No doubt he had written, but he had probably omitted to post the letter.

"Dear, dear!" said Mrs. McCrae.

At nine o'clock she made herself three pancakes with the pancake batter. The sole she put carefully away in the Frigidaire. "I wonder where the good man's got to now," she said to herself. She knew by experience that he might be anywhere. The odds were that he would discover his mistake in time to telegraph her or telephone her before she retired to bed. "I shall sit up until eleven o'clock but no longer," said Mrs. McCrae. Ten-thirty was her bedtime, an extension to eleven she considered her duty, but if at eleven there was nothing, no word from the canon, then Mrs. Mc-Crae would duly lock up the house and betake herself to bed.

It cannot be said that she was worried. This sort of thing had happened before. There was nothing to be done but wait for news of some kind. The possibilities were numerous. Canon Pennyfather might have got on the wrong train and failed to discover his misake until he was at Land's End or John o' Groats' or he might still be in London having made some mistake in the date, and was therefore convinced he was not returning until tomorrow. He might have met a friend or friends at this foreign conference he was going to and been induced to stay out there perhaps over the weekend. He would have meant to let her know but had entirely forgotten to do so. So, as has been already said, she was not worried. The day after tomorrow his old friend, Archdeacon Simmons, was coming to stay. That was the sort of thing the canon *did* remember, so no doubt he himself or a telegram from him would arrive tomorrow and at latest he would be home on the day after, or there would be a letter.

The morning of the day after, however, arrived without a word from him. For the first time Mrs. McCrae began to be uneasy. Between nine A.M. and one P.M. she eyed the telephone in a doubtful manner. Mrs. McCrae had her own fixed views about the telephone. She used it and recognized its convenience but she was not fond of the telephone. Some of her household shopping was done by telephone, though she much preferred to do it in person owing to a fixed belief that if you did not see what you were being given, a shopkeeper was sure to try and cheat you. Still, telephones were useful for domestic matters. She occasionally, though rarely, telephoned her friends or relations in the near neighbourhood. To make a call of any distance, or a London call, upset her severely. It was a shameful waste of money. Nevertheless, she began to meditate facing that problem.

Finally, when yet another day dawned without any news of him she decided to act. She knew where the canon was staying in London. Bertram's Hotel. A nice old-fashioned place. It might be as well, perhaps, if she rang up and made certain inquiries. They would probably know where the canon was. It was not an ordinary hotel. She would ask to be put through to Miss Gorringe. Miss Gorringe was always efficient and thoughtful. The canon might, of course, return by the twelve-thirty. If so he would be here any minute now.

But the minutes passed and there was no canon. Mrs. McCrae took a deep breath, nerved herself and asked for a call to London. She waited, biting her lips and holding the receiver clamped firmly to her ear.

"Bertram's Hotel, at your service," said the voice.

"I would like, if you please, to speak to Miss Gorringe," said Mrs. McCrae.

"Just a moment. What name shall I say?"

"It's Canon Pennyfather's housekeeper. Mrs. McCrae."

"Just a moment please."

Presently the calm and efficient voice of Miss Gorringe came through. "Miss Gorringe here. Did you say Canon Pennyfather's housekeeper?"

"That's right. Mrs. McCrea."

"Oh yes. Of course. What can I do for you, Mrs. McCrae?"

"Is Canon Pennyfather staying at the hotel still?"

"I'm glad you've wrung up," said Miss Gorringe. "We have been rather worried as to what exactly to do."

"Do you mean something's happened to Canon Pennyfather? Has he had an accident?"

"No, no, nothing of that kind. But we expected him back from Lucerne on Friday or Saturday."

"Eh—that'd be right."

"But he didn't arrive. Well, of course that wasn't really surprising. He had booked his room on—booked it, that is, until yesterday. He didn't come back yesterday or send any word and his things are still here. The major part of his baggage. We hadn't been quite sure what to do about it. Of course," Miss Gorringe went on hastily, "we know the canon is, well—somewhat forgetful sometimes."

"You may well say that!"

"It makes it a little difficult for us. We are so fully booked up. His room is actually booked for another guest." She added, "You have no idea where he is?"

With bitterness Mrs. McCrae said, "The man might

be anywhere!" She pulled herself together. "Well, thank you, Miss Gorringe."

"Anything I can do—" Miss Gorringe suggested helpfully.

"I daresay I'll hear soon enough," said Mrs. Mc-Crae. She thanked Miss Gorringe again and rang off.

She sat by the telephone, looking upset. She did not fear for the canon's personal safety. If he had had an accident, she would by now have been notified. She felt sure of that. On the whole the canon was not what one would call accident prone. He was what Mrs. McCrae called to herself "one of the scatty ones," and the scatty ones seemed always to be looked after by a special providence. While taking no care or thought, they could still survive even a Panda crossing. No, she did not visualize Canon Pennyfather as lying groaning in a hospital. He was somewhere, no doubt innocently and happily prattling with some friend or other. Maybe he was abroad still. The difficulty was that Archdeacon Simmons was arriving this evening and Archdeacon Simmons would expect to find a host to receive him. She couldn't put Archdeacon Simmons off because she didn't know where he was. It was all very difficult, but it had, like most difficulties, its bright spot. Its bright spot was Archdeacon Simmons. Archdeacon Simmons would know what to do. She would place the matter in his hands.

Archdeacon Simmons was a complete contrast to her employer. He knew where he was going, and what he was doing, and was always cheerfully sure of knowing the right thing to be done and doing it. A confident cleric. Archdeacon Simmons, when he arrived, to be met by Mrs. McCrea's explanations, apologies and perturbation, was a tower of strength. He, too, was not alarmed.

"Now don't you worry, Mrs. McCrae," he said in his genial fashion, as he sat down to the meal she had prepared for his arrival. "We'll hunt the absent-minded fellow down. Ever heard that story about Chesterton? G. K. Chesterton, you know, the writer. Wired to his wife when he'd gone on a lecture tour 'Am at Crewe Station. Where ought I to be?' "

He laughed. Mrs. McCrae smiled dutifully. She did not think it was very funny because it was so exactly the sort of thing that Canon Pennyfather might have done.

"Ah," said Archdeacon Simmons, with appreciation, "one of your excellent veal cutlets! You're a marvellous cook, Mrs. McCrae. I hope my old friend appreciates you."

Veal cutlets having been succeeded by some small castle puddings with a blackberry sauce which Mrs. McCrae had remembered was one of the archdeacon's favourite sweets, the good man applied himself in earnest to the tracking down of his missing friend. He addressed himself to the telephone with vigour and a complete disregard for expense, which made Mrs. McCrae purse her lips anxiously, although not really disapproving, because definitely her master had to be tracked down.

Having first dutifully tried the canon's sister who took little notice of her brother's goings and comings and as usual had not the faintest idea where he was or might be, the archdeacon spread his net farther afield. He addressed himself once more to Bertram's Hotel and got details as precisely as possible. The canon had definitely left there on the early evening of the nineteenth. He had with him a small B.E.A. handbag, but his other luggage had remained behind in his room, which he had duly retained. He had mentioned that he was going to a conference of some kind at Lucerne. He had not gone direct to the airport from the hotel. The commissionaire, who knew him well by sight, had put him into a taxi and had directed it as told by the canon, to the Athenaeum Club. That was the last time that anyone at Bertram's Hotel had seen Canon Penny-father. Oh yes, a small detail—he had omitted to leave his key behind but had taken it with him. It was not the first time that that had happened.

Archdeacon Simmons paused for a few minutes' consideration before the next call. He could ring up the airlines in London. That would no doubt take some time. There might be a short cut. He rang up Dr. Weissgarten, a learned Hebrew scholar who was almost certain to have been at the conference.

Dr. Weissgarten was at his home. As soon as he heard who was speaking to him he launched out into a torrent of verbiage consisting mostly of disparaging criticism of two papers that had been read at the conference in Lucerne.

"Most unsound, that fellow Hogarov," he said, "most unsound. How he gets away with it I don't know! Fellow isn't a scholar at all. Do you know what he actually said?"

The archdeacon sighed and had to be firm with him. Otherwise there was a good chance that the rest of the evening would be spent in listening to criticism of fellow scholars at the Lucerne Conference. With some reluctance Dr. Weissgarten was pinned down to more personal matters.

"Pennyfather?" he said, "Pennyfather? He ought to have been there. Can't think why he wasn't there. Said he was going. Told me only a week before when I saw him in the Athenaeum."

"You mean he wasn't at the conference at all?"

"That's what I've just said. He ought to have been there."

"Do you know why he wasn't there? Did he send an excuse?"

"How should I know? He certainly talked about being there. Yes, now I remember. He was expected. Several people remarked on his absence. Thought he might have had a chill or something. Very treacherous weather." He was about to revert to his criticisms of his fellow scholars but Archdeacon Simmons rang off.

He had got a fact but it was a fact that for the first time awoke in him an uneasy feeling. Canon Pennyfather had not been at the Lucerne Conference. He had meant to go to that conference. It seemed very extraordinary to the Archdeacon that he had not been there. He might, of course, have taken the wrong plane, though on the whole, B.E.A. were pretty careful of you and shepherded you away from such possibilities. Could Canon Pennyfather have forgotten the actual day that he was going to the conference? It was always possible, he supposed. But if so where had he gone instead?

He addressed himself now to the air terminal. It involved a great deal of patient waiting and being transferred from department to department. In the end he got a definite fact. Canon Pennyfather had booked as a passenger on the 21:40 plane to Lucerne on the eighteenth but he had not been on the plane.

"We're getting on," said Archdeacon Simmons to Mrs. McCrae, who was hovering in the background. "Now, let me see. Who shall I try next?"

"All this telephoning will cost a fearful lot of money," said Mrs. McCrea.

"I'm afraid so. I'm afraid so," said Archdeacon Simmons. "But we've got to get on his track, you know. He's not a very young man."

"Oh, sir, you don't think there's anything could really have happened to him?"

"Well I hope not. . . . I don't think so, because I think you'd have heard if so. He—er—always had his name and address on him, didn't he?"

"Oh yes, sir, he had cards on him. He'd have letters, too, and all sorts of things in his wallet."

"Well, I don't think he's in a hospital then," said the archdeacon. "Let me see. When he left the hotel he took a taxi to the Athenaeum. I'll ring them up next."

Here he got some definite information. Canon Pennyfather, who was well known there, had dined there at seven-thirty on the evening of the nineteenth. It was then that the archdeacon was struck by something he had overlooked until then. The aeroplane ticket had been for the eighteenth but the canon had left Bertram's Hotel by taxi to the Athenaeum, having mentioned he was going to the Lucerne Conference, on the nineteenth. Light began to break. Silly old ass, thought Archdeacon Simmons to himself, but careful not to say it aloud in front of Mrs. McCrae. "Got his dates wrong. The conference was on the nineteenth. I'm sure of it. He must have thought that he was leaving on the eighteenth. He was one day wrong."

He went over the next bit carefully. The canon would have gone to the Athenaeum, he would have dined, he would have gone on to Kensington Air Station. There, no doubt, it would have been pointed out to him that his ticket was for the day before and he would then have realized that the conference he was going to attend was now over.

"That's what happened," said Archdeacon Simmons, "depend upon it." He explained it to Mrs. McCrea, who agreed that it was likely enough. "Then what would he do?"

"Go back to his hotel," said Mrs. McCrae.

"He wouldn't have come straight down here—gone straight to the station, I mean."

"Not if his luggage was at the hotel. At any rate, he would have called there for his luggage."

"True enough," said Simmons. "All right. We'll think of it like this. He left the airport with his little bag and he went back to the hotel, or started for the hotel at all events. He might have had dinner perhaps —no, he'd dined at the Athenaeum. All right, he went back to the hotel. But he never arrived there." He paused a moment or two and then said doubtfully, "Or did he? Nobody seems to have seen him there. So what happened to him on the way?"

"He could have met someone," said Mrs. McCrae, doubtfully.

"Yes. Of course that's perfectly possible. Some old friend he hadn't seen for a long time. . . . He could have gone off with a friend to the friend's hotel or the friend's house, but he wouldn't have stayed there three days, would he? He wouldn't have forgotten for three whole days that his luggage was at the hotel. He'd have rung up about it, he'd have called for it, or in a supreme fit of absent-mindedness he might have come straight home. Three days' silence. That's what's so inexplicable."

"If he had an accident—"

"Yes, Mrs. McCrae, of course that's possible. We can try the hospitals. You say he had plenty of papers on him to identify him? Hm—I think there's only one thing for it."

Mrs. McCrae looked at him apprehensively.

"I think, you know," said the archdeacon gently, "that we've got to go to the police."

12

Miss Marple had found no difficulty in enjoying her stay in London. She did a lot of the things that she had not had the time to do in her hitherto brief visits to the capital. It has to be regretfully noted that she did not avail herself of the wide cultural activities that would have been possible to her. She visited no picture galleries and no museums. The idea of patronizing a dress show of any kind would not even have occurred to her. What she did visit were the glass and china departments of the large stores, and the household lined departments, and she also availed herself of some marked down lines in furnishing fabrics. Having spent what she considered a reasonable sum upon these household investments, she indulged in various excursions of her own. She went to places and shops she remembered from her young days, sometimes merely with the curiosity of seeing whether they were still there. It was not a pursuit that she had ever had time for before, and she enjoyed it very much. After a nice little nap after lunch, she would go out, and, avoiding the attentions of the commissionaire if possible, because he was so firmly imbued with the idea that a lady of her age and frailty should always go in a taxi, she walked towards a bus stop, or tube station.

She had bought a small guide to buses and their routes —and an underground transport map; and she would plan her excursion carefully. One afternoon she could be seen walking happily and nostalgically around Evelyn Gardens or Onslow Square murmuring softly, "Yes, that was Mrs. Van Dylan's house. Of course it looks quite different now. They seem to have remodelled it. Dear me, I see it's got four bells. Four flats, I suppose. Such a nice old-fashioned square this always was."

Rather shamefacedly she paid a visit to Madame Tussaud's, a well-remembered delight of her childhood. In Westbourne Grove she looked in vain for Bradley's. Aunt Helen had always gone to Bradley's about her sealskin jacket.

Window shopping in the general sense did not interest Miss Marple, but she had a splendid time rounding up knitting patterns, new varieties of knitting wool, and suchlike delights. She made a special expedition to Richmond to see the house that had been occupied by Great-Uncle Thomas, the retired admiral. The handsome terrace was still there but here again each house seemed to be turned into flats. Much more painful was the house in Lowndes Square where a distant cousin, Lady Merridew, had lived in some style. Here a vast skyscraper building of modernistic design appeared to have arisen. Miss Marple shook her head sadly and said firmly to herself, "There must be progress I suppose. If Cousin Ethel knew, she'd turn in her grave, I'm sure."

It was one particularly mild and pleasant afternoon that Miss Marple embarked on a bus that took her over Battersea Bridge. She was going to combine the double pleasure of taking a sentimental look at Princes Terrace Mansions where an old governess of hers had once lived, and visiting Battersea Park. The first part of her quest was abortive. Miss Ledbury's former home had vanished without trace and had been replaced by a great deal of gleaming concrete. Miss Marple turned into Battersea Park. She had always been a good walker but had to admit that nowadays her walking powers were not what they were. Half a mile was quite enough to tire her. She could manage, she thought, to cross the Park and go out over Chelsea Bridge and find herself once more on a convenient bus route, but her steps grew gradually slower and slower, and she was pleased to come upon a tea enclosure situated on the edge of the lake.

Teas were still being served there in spite of the autumn chill. There were not many people today, a certain amount of mothers and prams, and a few pairs of young lovers. Miss Marple collected a tray with tea and two sponge cakes. She carried her tray carefully to a table and sat down. The tea was just what she needed. Hot, strong and very reviving. Revived, she looked round her, and her eyes stopping suddenly at a particular table, she sat up very straight in her chair. Really, a very strange coincidence, very strange indeed! First the Army and Navy Stores and now here. Very unusual places those particular two people chose! But no! She was wrong. Miss Marple took a second and stronger pair of glasses from her bag. Yes, she had been mistaken. There was a certain similarity, of course. That long straight blonde hair; but this was not Bess Sedgwick. It was someone years younger. Of course! It was the daughter! The young girl who had come into Bertram's with Lady Selina Hazy's friend, Colonel Luscombe. But the man was the same man who had been lunching with Lady Sedgwick in the Army and Navy Stores. No doubt about it, the same handsome, hawk-like look, the same leanness, the same predatory toughness and—yes, the same strong, virile attraction.

"Bad!" said Miss Marple. "Bad all through! Cruel! Unscrupulous. I don't like seeing this. First the mother, now the daughter. What does it mean?"

It meant no good. Miss Marple's was sure of that. Miss Marple seldom gave anyone the benefit of the doubt; she invariably thought the worst, and nine times out of ten, so she insisted, she was right in so doing. Both these meetings, she was sure, were more or less secret meetings. She observed now the way these two bent forward over the table until their heads nearly touched, and the earnestness with which they talked. The girl's face—Miss Marple took off her spectacles, rubbed the lenses carefully, then put them on again. Yes, this girl was in love. Desperately in love, as only the young can be in love. But what were her guardians about to let her run about London and have these clandestine assignments in Battersea Park? A nicely brought up, well-behaved girl like that. Too nicely brought up, no doubt! Her people probably believed her to be in some quite other spot. She had to tell lies.

On her way out Miss Marple passed the table where they were sitting, slowing down as much as she could without its being too obvious. Unfortunately, their voices were so low that she could not hear what they said. The man was speaking, the girl was listening, half pleased, half afraid. Planning to run away together, perhaps? thought Miss Marple. She's still under age.

Miss Marple passed through the small gate in the

fence that led to the sidewalk of the park. There were cars parked along there and presently she stopped beside one particular car. Miss Marple was not particularly knowledgeable over cars but such cars as this one did not come her way very often, so she had noted and remembered it. She had acquired a little information about cars of this style from an enthusiastic great-nephew. It was a racing car. Some foreign make —she couldn't remember the name now. Not only that, she had seen this car or one exactly like it, seen it only yesterday in a side street close to Bertram's Hotel. She had noticed it not only because of its size and its powerful and unusual appearance but because the number had awakened some vague memory, some trace of association in her memory. FAN 2266. It had made her think of her cousin Fanny Godfrey. Poor Fanny who stuttered, who had said, "I have got t-t-two s-s-s-potz. . . ."

She walked along and looked at the number of this car. Yes, she was quite right. FAN 2266. It was the same car. Miss Marple, her footsteps growing more painful every moment, arrived deep in thought at the other side of Chelsea Bridge and by then was so exhausted that she hailed the first taxi she saw with decision. She was worried by the feeling that there was something she ought to do about things. But what things and what to do about them? It was all so indefinite. She fixed her eyes absently on some newsboards.

SENSATIONAL DEVELOPMENTS IN TRAIN ROBBERY, they ran. ENGINE DRIVER'S STORY, said another one. Really! Miss Marple thought to herself, every day there seemed to be a bank holdup or a train robbery or a wage pay snatch.

Crime seemed to have got above itself.

13

Vaguely reminiscent of a large bumblebee, Chief Inspector Fred Davy wandered around the confines of the Criminal Investigation Department, humming to himself. It was a well-known idiosyncrasy of his, and caused no particular notice except to give rise to the remark that "Father was on the prowl again."

His prowling led him at last to the room where Inspector Campbell was sitting behind a desk with a bored expression. Inspector Campbell was an ambitious young man and he found much of his occupation tedious in the extreme. Nevertheless, he coped with the duties appointed to him and achieved a very fair measure of success in so doing. The powers that be approved of him, thought he should do well and doled out from time to time a few words of encouraging commendation.

"Good morning, sir," said Inspector Campbell, respectfully, when Father entered his domain. Naturally he called Chief Inspector Davy "Father" behind his back as everyone else did; but he was not yet of sufficient seniority to do such a thing to his face.

"Anything I can do for you, sir?" he inquired.

"La, la, boom, boom," hummed the Chief Inspector,

slightly off key. "Why must they call me Mary when my name's Miss Gibbs?" After this rather unexpected resurrection of a bygone musical comedy, he drew up a chair and sat down. "Busy?" he asked.

"Moderately so."

"Got some disappearance case or other on, haven't you, to do with some hotel or other? What's the name of it now? Bertram's. Is that it?"

"Yes, that's right, sir. Bertram's Hotel."

"Oh no, sir," said Inspector Campbell, slightly shocked at hearing Bertram's Hotel being referred to in such a connection. "Very nice, quiet, old-fashioned place."

"Is it now?" said Father. "Yes, is it now? Well, that's interesting, really."

Inspector Campbell wondered why it was interesting. He did not like to ask, as tempers in the upper hierarchy were notoriously short since the mail train robbery, which had been a spectacular success for the criminals. He looked at Father's large, heavy, bovine face and wondered, as he had once or twice wondered before, how Chief Inspector Davy had reached his present rank and why he was so highly thought of in the department. All right in his day, I suppose, thought Inspector Campbell, but there are plenty of go-ahead chaps about who could do with some promotion, once the deadwood is cleared away. But the deadwood had begun another song, partly hummed, with an occasional word or two here and there.

"Tell me, gentle stranger, are there any more at home like you?" intoned Father and then in a sudden falsetto, "A few, kind sir, and nicer girls you never knew. No, let's see, I've got the sexes mixed up. *Floradora*. That was a good show, too."

"I believe I've heard of it, sir," said Inspector Campbell.

"Your mother sang you to sleep in the cradle with it, I expect," said Chief Inspector Davy. "Now then, what's been going on at Bertram's Hotel? Who has disappeared and how and why?"

"A Canon Pennyfather, sir. Elderly clergyman."

"Dull case, eh?"

Inspector Campbell smiled. "Yes, sir, it is rather dull in a way."

"What did he look like?"

"Canon Pennyfather?"

"Yes—you've got a description, I suppose?"

"Of course." Campbell shuffled papers and read: "Height five feet eight. Large thatch of white hair—stoops . . ."

"And he disappeared from Bertram's Hotel—when?"

"About a week ago—November nineteenth."

"And they've just reported it. Took their time about it, didn't they?"

"Well, I think there was a general idea that he'd turn up."

"Any idea what's behind it?" asked Father. "Has a decent God-fearing man suddenly gone off with one of the churchwardens' wives? Or does he do a bit of secret drinking, or has he embezzled the church funds? Or is he the sort of absent-minded old chap who goes in for this sort of thing?"

"Well, from all I can hear, sir, I should say the latter. He's done it before."

"What—disappeared from a respectable West End hotel?"

"No, not exactly that, but he's not always returned home when he was expected. Occasionally he's turned up to stay with friends on a day when they haven't asked him, or not turned up on the date when they had asked him. That sort of thing."

"Yes," said Father. "Yes. Well that sounds very nice and natural and according to plan, doesn't it? When exactly did you say he disappeared?"

"Thursday. November nineteenth. He was supposed to be attending a congress at"—he bent down and studied some papers on his desk—"oh yes, Lucerne. Society of Biblical Historical Studies. That's the English translation of it. I think it's actually a German society."

"And it was held at Lucerne? The old boy—I suppose he is an old boy?"

"Sixty-three, sir, I understand."

"The old boy didn't turn up, is that it?"

Inspector Campbell drew his papers towards him and gave Father the ascertainable facts in so far as they had been ascertained.

"Doesn't sound as if he'd gone off with a choirboy," observed Chief Inspector Davy.

"I expect he'll turn up all right," said Campbell, "but we're looking into it, of course. Are you—er—particularly interested in the case, sir?" He could hardly restrain his curiosity on this point.

"No," said Davy thoughtfully. "No, I'm not interested in the case. I don't see anything to be interested about in it."

There was a pause, a pause which clearly contained the words "Well, then?" with a question mark after it from Inspector Campbell, which he was too well trained to utter in audible tones.

"What I'm really interested in," said Father, "is the date. And Bertram's Hotel, of course."

"It's always been very well conducted, sir. No trouble there."

"That's very nice, I'm sure," said Father. He added

thoughtfully, "I'd rather like to have a look at the place."

"Of course, sir," said Inspector Campbell. "Any time you like. I was thinking of going round there myself."

"I might as well come along with you," said Father. "Not to butt in, nothing like that. But I'd just rather like to have a look at the place, and this disappearing archdeacon of yours, or whatever he is, makes rather a good excuse. No need to call me 'sir' when we're there —you throw your weight about. I'll just be your stooge."

Inspector Campbell became interested.

"Do you think there's something that might tie in there, sir, something that might tie in with something else?"

"There's no reason to believe so, so far," said Father. "But you know how it is. One gets—I don't know what to call them—whims, do you think? Bertram's Hotel, somehow, sounds almost too good to be true."

He resumed his impersonation of a bumble bee with a rendering of "Let's All Go Down the Strand."

The two detective officers went off together, Campbell looking smart in a lounge suit (he had an excellent figure), and Chief Insepector Davy carrying with him a tweedy air of being up from the country. They fitted in quite well. Only the astute eye of Miss Gorringe, as she raised it from her ledgers, singled them out and appreciated them for what they were. Since she had reported the disappearance of Canon Pennyfather herself and had already had a word with a lesser personage in the police force, she had been expecting somthing of this kind.

A faint murmur to the earnest-looking girl assistant

whom she kept handy in the background, enabled the latter to come forward and deal with any ordinary inquiries or services while Miss Gorringe gently shifted herself a little farther along the counter and looked up at the two men. Inspector Campbell laid down his card on the desk in front of her and she nodded. Looking past him to the large tweed-coated figure behind him, she noted that he had turned slightly sideways, and was observing the lounge and its occupants with an apparently naïve pleasure at beholding such a well-bred, upper-class world in action.

"Would you like to come into the office?" said Miss Gorringe. "We can talk better there perhaps."

"Yes, I think that would be best."

"Nice place you've got here," said the large, fat, bovine-looking man, turning his head back towards her. "Comfortable," he added, looking approvingly at the large fire. "Good old-fashioned comfort."

Miss Gorringe smiled with an air of pleasure.

"Yes indeed. We pride ourselves on making our vistors comfortable," she said. She turned to her assistant. "Will you carry on, Alice? There is the ledger. Lady Jocelyn will be arriving quite soon. She is sure to want to change her room as soon as she sees it but you must explain to her we are really full up. If necessary, you can show her number 340 on the third floor and offer her that instead. It's not a very pleasant room and I'm sure she will be content with her present one as soon as she sees that."

"Yes, Miss Gorringe. I'll do just that, Miss Gorringe."

"And remind Colonel Mortimer that his field glasses are here. He asked me to keep them for him this morning. Don't let him go off without them."

"No, Miss Gorringe."

These duties accomplished, Miss Gorringe looked at the two men, came out from behind the desk and walked along to a plain mahogany door with no legend on it. Miss Gorringe opened it and they went into a small, rather sad-looking office. All three sat down.

"The missing man is Canon Pennyfather, I understand," said Inspector Campbell. He looked at his notes. "I've got Sergeant Wadell's report. Perhaps you'll tell me in your own words just what occurred."

"I don't think that Canon Pennyfather has really disappeared in the sense in which one would usually use that word," said Miss Gorringe. "I think, you know, that he's just met someone somewhere, some old friend or something like that, and had perhaps gone off with him to some scholarly meeting or reunion or something of that kind, on the Continent. He is so very vague."

"You've known him for a long time?"

"Oh yes, he's been coming here to stay for—let me see—oh five or six years at least, I should think."

"You've been here some time yourself, ma'am," said Chief Inspector Davy, suddenly putting in a word.

"I have been here, let me think, fourteen years," said Miss Gorringe.

"It's a nice place," repeated Davy again. "And Canon Pennyfather usually stayed here when he was in London? Is that right?"

"Yes. He always came to us. He wrote well beforehand to retain his room. He was much less vague on paper than he was in real life. He asked for a room from the seventeenth to the twenty-first. During that time he expected to be away for one or two nights, and he explained that he wished to keep his room on while he was away. He quite often did that."

"When did you begin to get worried about him?" asked Campbell.

"Well, I didn't really. Of course it was awkward. You see, his room was let on from the twenty-third and when I realized—I didn't at first—that he hadn't come back from Lugano—"

"I've got Lucerne here in my notes," said Campbell.

"Yes, yes, I think it was Lucerne. Some archaeological congress or other. Anyway, when I realized he hadn't come back here and that his baggage was still here waiting in his room, it made things rather awkward. You see, we are very booked up at this time of year and I had someone else coming into his room. The Honourable Mrs. Saunders, who lives at Lyme Regis. She always had that room. And then his housekeeper rang up. She was worried."

"The housekeeper's name is Mrs. McCrae, so I understand from Archdeacon Simmons. Do you know her?"

"Not personally, no, but I have spoken to her on the telephone once or twice. She is, I think, a very reliable woman and has been with Canon Pennyfather for some years. She was worried naturally. I believe she and Archdeacon Simmons got in touch with near friends and relations but they knew nothing of Canon Pennyfather's movements. And since he was expecting the archdeacon to stay with him it certainly seemed very odd—in fact it still does—that the canon should not have returned home."

"Is this canon usually as absent-minded as that?" asked Father.

Miss Corringe ignored him. This large man, presumably the accompanying sergeant, seemed to her to be pushing himself forward a little too much.

"And now I understand," continued Miss Gorringe,

in an annoyed voice, "and now I understand from Archdeacon Simmons that the canon never even went to this conference in Lucerne."

"Did he send any message to say he wouldn't go."

"I don't think so—not from here. No telegram of anything like that. I really know nothing about Lucerne —I am really only concerned with our side of the matter. It has got into the evening papers, I see—the fact that he is missing, I mean. They haven't mentioned he was staying here. I hope they won't. We don't want the press here, our visitors wouldn't like that at all. If you can keep them off us, Inspector Campbell, we should be very grateful. I mean it's not as if he had disappeared from here."

"His luggage is still here?"

"Yes. In the baggage room. If he didn't go to Lucerne, have you considered the possibility of his being run over? Something like that?"

"Nothing like that has happened to him."

"It really does seem very, very curious," said Miss Gorringe, a faint flicker of interest appearing in her manner, to replace the annoyance. "I mean, it does make one wonder where he could have gone and why?"

Father looked at her comprehendingly. "Of course," he said. "You've only been thinking of it from the hotel angle. Very natural."

"I understand," said Inspector Campbell, referring once more to his notes, "that Canon Pennyfather left here about six-thirty on the evening of Thursday the nineteenth. He had with him a small overnight bag and he left here in a taxi, directing the commissionaire to tell the driver to drive to the Athenaeum Club."

Miss Gorringe nodded her head. "Yes, he dined at

the Athenaeum Club—Archdeacon Simmons told me that that was the place he was last seen."

There was a firmness in Miss Gorringe's voice as she transferred the responsibility of seeing the canon last from Bertram's Hotel to the Athenaeum Club.

"Well, it's nice to get the facts straight," said Father in a gentle rumbling voice. "We've got 'em straight now. He went off with his little blue B.O.A.C. bag or whatever he'd got with him—it was a blue B.O.A.C. bag, yes? He went off and he didn't come back, and that's that."

"So you see, really I cannot help you," said Miss Gorringe, showing a disposition to rise to her feet and get back to work.

"It doesn't seem as if you could help us," said Father, "but someone else might be able to," he added.

"Someone else?"

"Why, yes," said Father. "One of the staff perhaps."

"I don't think anyone knows anything; or they would certainly have reported it to me."

"Well, perhaps they might. Perhaps they mightn't. What I mean is, they'd have told you if they'd distinctly known anything. But I was thinking more of something he might have said."

"What sort of thing?" said Miss Gorringe, looking perplexed.

"Oh, just some chance word that might give one a clue. Something like 'I'm going to see an old friend to-night that I haven't seen since we met in Arizona.' Something like that. Or 'I'm going to stay next week with a niece of mine for her daughter's confirmation.' With absent-minded people, you know, clues like that are a great help. They show what was in the person's mind. It may be that after his dinner at the Athenaeum, he gets into a taxi and thinks 'Now where am I going?' and having got—say—the confirmation in his mind—thinks he's going off there."

"Well, I see what you mean," said Miss Gorringe doubtfully. "It seems a little unlikely."

"Oh, one never knows one's luck," said Father cheerfully. "Then there are the various guests here. I suppose Canon Pennyfather knew some of them since he came here fairly often."

"Oh yes," said Miss Gorringe, "Let me see now. I've seen him talking to—yes, Lady Selina Hazy. Then there was the Bishop of Norwich. They're old friends, I believe. They were at Oxford together. And Mrs. Jameson and her daughters. They come from the same part of the world. Oh yes, quite a lot of people."

"You see," said Father, "he might have talked to one of them. He might have just mentioned some little thing that would give us a clue. Is there anyone staying here now that the canon knew fairly well?"

Miss Gorringe frowned in thought. "Well, I think General Radley is here still. And there's an old lady who came up from the country—who used to stay here as a girl, so she told me. Let me see, I can't remember her name at the moment, but I can find it for you. Oh yes, Miss Marple, that's her name. I believe she knew him."

"Well, we could make a start with those two. And there'd be a chambermaid, I suppose."

"Oh yes," said Miss Gorringe. "But she has been interviewed already by Sergeant Wadell."

"I know. But not perhaps from this angle. What about the waiter who attended on his table. Or the head waiter?"

"There's Henry, of course," said Miss Gorringe.

"Who's Henry?" asked Father.

Miss Gorringe looked almost shocked. It was to her impossible that anyone should not know Henry.

"Henry had been here for more years than I can say," she said. "You must have noticed him serving teas as you came in."

"Kind of personality," said Davy. "I remember noticing him."

"I don't know what we should do without Henry," said Miss Gorringe with feeling. "He really is wonderful. He sets the tone of the place, you know."

"Perhaps he might like to serve some tea to me," said Chief Inspector Davy. "Muffins, I saw he'd got there. I'd like a good muffin again."

"Certainly if you like," said Miss Gorringe, rather coldly. "Shall I order two teas to be served to you in the lounge?" she added, turning to Inspector Campbell.

"That would—" the inspector began, when suddenly the door opened and Mr. Humfries appeared in his Olympian manner.

He looked slightly taken aback, then looked inquiringly at Miss Gorringe. Miss Gorringe explained.

"These are two gentlemen from Scotland Yard, Mr. Humfries," she said.

"Detective Inspector Campbell," said Campbell.

"Oh yes. Yes, of course," said Mr. Humfries. "The matter of Canon Pennyfather, I suppose? Most extraordinary business. I hope nothing's happened to him, poor old chap."

"So do I," said Miss Gorringe. "Such a dear old man."

"One of the old school," said Mr. Humfries approvingly.

"You seem to have quite a lot of the old school here," observed Chief Inspector Davy.

"I suppose we do, I suppose we do," said Mr. Humfries. "Yes, in many ways we are quite a survival."

"We have our regulars, you know," said Miss Gorringe. She spoke proudly. "The same people come back year after year. We have a lot of Americans. People from Boston, and Washington. Very quiet, nice people."

"They like our English atmosphere," said Mr. Humfries, showing his very white teeth in a smile.

Father looked at him thoughtfully.

Inspector Campbell said, "You're quite sure that no message came here from the canon? I mean it might have been taken by someone who forgot to write it down or to pass it on."

"Telephone messages are always taken down most carefully," said Miss Gorringe with ice in her voice. "I cannot conceive it possible that a message would not have been passed on to me or to the appropriate person on duty."

She glared at him.

Inspector Campbell looked momentarily taken aback.

"We've really answered all these questions before, you know," said Mr. Humfries, also with a touch of ice in his voice. "We gave all the information at our disposal to your sergeant—I can't remember his name for the moment."

Father stirred a little and said, in a kind of homely way, "Well you see, things have begun to look rather more serious. It looks like a bit more than absentmindedness. That's why, I think, it would be a good thing if we could have a word or two with those two people you mentioned—General Radley and Miss Marple."

"You want me to—to arrange an interview with them? Mr. Humfries looked rather unhappy. "General Radley's very deaf."

"I don't think it will be necessary to make it too formal," said Chief Inspector Davy. "We don't want to worry people. You can leave it quite safely to us. Just point out those two you mentioned. There is just a chance you know, that Canon Pennyfather might have mentioned some plan of his, or some person he was going to meet at Lucerne or who was going with him to Lucerne. Anyway, it's worth trying."

Mr. Humfries looked somewhat relieved. "Nothing more we can do for you?" he asked. "I'm sure you understand that we wish to help you in every way, only you do understand how we feel about any press publicity."

"Quite," said Inspector Campbell.

"And I'll just have a word with the chambermaid," said Father.

"Certainly, if you like. I doubt very much whether she can tell you anything."

"Probably not. But there might be some detail— some remark the canon made about a letter or an appointment. One never knows."

Mr. Humfries glanced at his watch. "She'll be on duty at six," he said. "Second floor. Perhaps in the meantime, you'd care for tea?"

"Suits me," said Father promptly.

They left the office together.

Miss Gorringe said, "General Radley will be in the smoking room. The first room down that passage on the left. He'll be in front of the fire there with *The Times*. I think," she added discreetly, "he might be asleep. You're sure you don't want me to—"

"No, no, I'll see to it," said Father. "And what about the other one—the old lady?"

"She's sitting over there, by the fireplace," said Miss Gorringe.

"The one with white fluffy hair and the knitting?" said Father, taking a look. "Might almost be on the stage, mightn't she? Everybody's universal great-aunt."

"Great aunts aren't much like that nowadays," said Miss Gorringe, "nor grandmothers nor great-grand-mothers, if it comes to that. We had the Marchioness of Barlowe in yesterday. She's a great-grandmother. Honestly, I didn't know her when she came in. Just back from Paris. Her face a mask of pink and white and her hair platinum blonde and I suppose an entirely false figure, but it looked wonderful."

"Ah," said Father, "I prefer the old-fashioned kind myself. Well, thank you, ma'am." He turned to Camp-bell. "I'll look after it, shall I, sir? I know you've got an important appointment."

"That's right," said Campbell, taking his cue. "I don't suppose anything much will come of it, but it's worth trying."

Mr. Humfries disappeared into his inner sanctum, saying as he did so, "Miss Gorringe—just a moment, please."

Miss Gorringe followed him in and shut the door behind her.

Humfries was walking up and down. "What do they want to see Rose for?" he demanded sharply. "Wadell asked all the necessary questions."

"I suppose it's just routine," said Miss Gorringe, doubtfully.

"You'd better have a word with her first."

Miss Gorringe looked a little startled. "But surely Inspector Campbell—"

"Oh, I'm not worried about Campbell. It's the other one. Do you know who he is?"

"I don't think he gave his name. Sergeant of some kind, I suppose. He looks rather a yokel."

"Yokel my foot," said Mr. Humfries, abandoning his elegance. "That's Chief Inspector Davy, and old fox if there ever was one. They think a lot of him at the Yard. I'd like to know what he's doing here, nosing about and playing the genial hick. I don't like it at all."

"You can't think—"

"I don't know what to think. But I tell you I don't like it. Did he ask to see anyone else besides Rose?"

"I think he's going to have a word with Henry." Mr. Humfries laughed. Miss Gorringe laughed too. "We needn't worry about Henry."

"No, indeed."

"And the visitors who knew Canon Pennyfather?" Mr. Humfries laughed again.

"I wish him joy of old Radley. He'll have to shout the place down and then he won't get anything worth having. He's welcome to Radley and that funny old hen, Miss Marple. All the same, I don't much like his poking his nose in. . . ."

14

"You know," said Chief Inspector Davy thoughtfully, "I don't much like that chap Humfries."

"Think there's something wrong with him?" asked Campbell.

"Well—" Father sounded apologetic, "you know the sort of feeling one gets. Smarmy sort of chap. I wonder if he's the owner or only manager."

"I could ask him." Campbell took a step back towards the desk.

"No, don't ask him," said Father. "Just find out—quietly."

Campbell looked at him curiously. "What's on your mind, sir?"

"Nothing in particular," said Father. "I just think I'd like to have a good deal more information about this place. I'd like to know who is behind it, what its financial status is. All that sort of thing."

Campbell shook his head. "I should have said if there was one place in London that was absolutely above suspicion—"

"I know, I know," said Father. "And what a useful thing it is to have that reputation!"

Campbell shook his head again and left. Father

went down the passage to the smoking room. General Radley was just waking up. *The Times* had slipped from his knees and disintegrated slightly. Father picked it up and reassembled the sheets and handed it to him.

"Thank ye, sir. Very kind," said General Radley gruffly.

"General Radley?"

"Yes."

"You'll excuse me," said Father, raising his voice, "but I want to speak to you about Canon Penny-father."

"Eh—what's that?" The general approached a hand to his ear.

"Canon Pennyfather," bellowed Father.

"My father? Dead years ago."

"Canon *Penny*-father."

"Oh. What about him? Saw him the other day. He was staying here."

"There was an address he was going to give me. Said he'd leave it with you."

This was rather more difficult to get over but he succeeded in the end.

"Never gave me any address. Must have mixed me up with somebody else. Muddle-headed old fool. Always was. Scholarly sort of chap, you know. They're always absent-minded."

Father perservered for a little longer but soon decided that conversation with General Radley was practically impossible and almost certainly unprofitable. He went and sat down in the lounge at a table adjacent to that of Miss Jane Marple.

"Tea, sir?"

Father looked up. He was impressed, as everyone was impressed by Henry's personality. Though such a large and portly man he had appeared, as it were, like some vast travesty of Ariel who could materialize and vanish at will. Father ordered tea.

"Did I see you've got muffins here?" he asked.

Henry smiled benignly. "Yes, sir. Very good indeed our muffins are, if I may say so. Everyone enjoys them. Shall I order you muffins, sir? Indian or China tea?"

"Indian," said Father. "Or Ceylon if you've got it."

"Certainly we have Ceylon, sir."

Henry made the faintest gesture with a finger and the pale young man who was his minion departed in search of Ceylon tea and muffins. Henry moved graciously elsewhere.

You're *someone,* you are, thought Father. I wonder where they got hold of you and what they pay you. A packet, I bet, and you'd been worth it. He watched Henry bending in a fatherly manner over an elderly lady. He wondered what Henry thought, if he thought anything, about Father. Father considered that he fitted into Bertram's Hotel reasonably well. He might have been a prosperous gentleman farmer or he might have been a peer of the realm with a resemblance to a bookmaker. Father knew two peers who were very like that. On the whole, he thought, he passed muster, but he also thought it possible that he had not deceived Henry. Yes, you're *someone,* you are, Father thought again.

Tea came and the muffins. Father bit deeply. Butter ran down his chin. He wiped it off with a large handkerchief. He drank two cups of tea with plenty of sugar. Then he leaned forward and spoke to the lady sitting in the chair next to him.

"Excuse me," he said, "but aren't you Miss Jane Marple?"

Miss Marple transferred her gaze from her knitting to Chief Detective Inspector Davy.

"Yes," she said, "I am Miss Marple."

"I hope you don't mind my speaking to you. As a matter of fact I am a police officer."

"Indeed? Nothing seriously wrong here, I hope?"

Father hastened to reassure her in his best paternal fashion.

"Now, don't you worry, Miss Marple," he said. "It's not the sort of thing you mean at all. No burglary or anything like that. Just a little difficulty about an absent-minded clergyman, that's all. I think he's a friend of yours. Canon Pennyfather."

"Oh, Canon Pennyfather. He was here only the other day. Yes, I've known him slightly for many years. As you say, he is very absent-minded." She added, with some interest, "What has he done now?"

"Well, as you might say in a manner of speaking, he's lost himself."

"Oh dear," said Miss Marple. "Where ought he to be?"

"Back at home in his Cathedral Close," said Father, "but he isn't."

"He told me," said Miss Marple, "he was going to a conference at Lucerne. Something to do with the Dead Sea scrolls, I believe. He's a great Hebrew and Aramaic scholar, you know."

"Yes," said Father. "You're quite right. That's where he—well, that's where he was supposed to be going."

"Do you mean he didn't turn up there?"

"No," said Father, "he didn't turn up."

"Oh, well," said Miss Marple, "I expect he got his dates wrong."

"Very likely, very likely."

"I'm afraid," said Miss Marple, "that that's not the first time that that's happened. I went to have tea with him in Chadminster once. He was actually absent

138

from home. His housekeeper told me then how very absent-minded he was."

"He didn't say anything to you when he was staying here that might give us a clue, I suppose?" asked Father, speaking in an easy and confidential way. "You know the sort of thing I mean, any old friend he'd met or any plans he'd made a part from this Lucerne Conference?"

"Oh no. He just mentioned the Lucerne Conference. I think he said it was on the nineteenth. Is that right?"

"That was the date of the Lucerne Conference, yes."

"I didn't notice the date particularly. I mean—" like most old ladies, Miss Marple here became slightly involved— "I thought he said the nineteenth and he might have meant the nineteenth and it might really have been the twentieth. I mean, he may have thought the twentieth was the nineteenth or he may have thought the nineteenth was the twentieth."

"Well—" said Father, slightly dazed.

"I'm putting it badly," said Miss Marple, "but I mean people like Canon Pennyfather, if they say they're going somewhere on a Thursday, one is quite prepared to find that they didn't mean Thursday, it may be Wednesday or Friday they really mean. Usually they find out in time but sometimes they just don't. I thought at the time that something like that must have happened."

Father looked slightly puzzled.

"You speak as though you knew already, Miss Marple, that Canon Pennyfather hadn't gone to Lucerne."

"I knew he wasn't in Lucerne on Thursday," said Miss Marple. "He was here all day—or most of the day. That's why I thought, of course, that though he may have said Thursday to me, it was really Friday he meant. He certainly left here on Thursday evening carrying his B.E.A. bag."

"Quite so."

"I took it he was going off to the airport then," said Miss Marple. "That's why I was so surprised to see he was back again."

"I beg your pardon, what do you mean by 'back again'?"

"Well, that he was back here again, I mean."

"Now, let's get this quite clear," said Father, careful to speak in an agreeable and reminiscent voice, and not as though it was really important. "You saw the old idio—you saw the canon, that is to say, leave as you thought for the airport with his overnight bag, fairly early in the evening. Is that right?"

"Yes. About half-past six, I would say, or quarter to seven."

"But you say he came back."

"Perhaps he missed the plane. That would account for it."

"When did he come back?"

"Well, I don't really know. I didn't see him come back."

"Oh," said Father, taken aback. "I thought you said you did see him."

"Oh, I did see him later," said Miss Marple, "I meant I didn't see him actually come into the hotel."

"You saw him later? When?"

Miss Marple thought.

"Let me see. It was about 3 A.M. I couldn't sleep very well. Something woke me. Some sound. There are so many queer noises in London. I looked at my little clock, it was ten minutes past three. For some reason—I'm not quite sure what—I felt uneasy. Footsteps, perhaps, outside my door. Living in the country, if one hears footsteps in the middle of the night it makes one nervous. So I just opened my door and looked out. There was Canon Pennyfather leaving his room—it's next door to mine—and going off down the stairs wearing his overcoat."

"He came out of his room wearing his overcoat and went down the stairs at three A.M. in the morning?"

"Yes," said Miss Marple and added: "I thought it odd at the time."

Father looked at her for some moments. "Miss Marple," he said, "why haven't you told anyone this before?"

"Nobody asked me," said Miss Marple simply.

15

Father drew a deep breath.

"No," he said. "No, I suppose nobody would ask you. It's as simple as that."

He relapsed into silence again.

"You think something has happened to him, don't you?" asked Miss Marple.

"It's over a week now," said Father. "He didn't have a stroke and fall down in the street. He's not in a hospital as a result of an accident. So where is he? His disappearance has been reported in the press, but nobody's come forward with any information yet."

"They may not have seen it. I didn't."

"It looks—it really looks—" Father was following out his own line of thought—"as though he meant to disappear. Leaving this place like that in the middle of the night. You're quite sure about it, aren't you?" he demanded sharply. "You didn't dream it?"

"I am absolutely sure," said Miss Marple with finality.

Father heaved himself to his feet. "I'd better go and see that chambermaid," he said.

Father found Rose Sheldon on duty and ran an approving eye over her pleasant person.

"I'm sorry to bother you," he said. "I know you've seen our sergeant already. But it's about that missing gentleman, Canon Pennyfather."

"Oh yes, sir, a very nice gentleman. He often stays here."

"Absent-minded," said Father.

Rose Sheldon permitted a discreet smile to appear on her respectful mask of a face.

"Now let me see." Father pretended to consult some notes. "The last time you saw Canon Penny-father—was—"

"On the Thursday morning, sir. Thursday the nine-teenth. He told me that he would not be back that night and possibly not the next either. He was going, I think, to Geneva. Somewhere in Switzerland, anyway. He gave me two shirts he wanted washed and I said they would be ready for him on the morning of the following day."

"And that's the last you saw of him, eh?"

"Yes, sir. You see, I'm not on duty in the afternoons. I come back again at six o'clock. By then he must have left, or at any rate he was downstairs. Not in his room. He had left two suitcases behind."

"That's right," said Father. The contents of the suit-cases had been examined, but had given no useful lead. He went on, "Did you call him the next morning?"

"Call him? No, sir, he was away."

"What did you do ordinarily—take him early tea? Breakfast?"

"Early tea, sir. He breakfasted downstairs always."

"So you didn't go into his room at all the next day?"

"Oh yes, sir." Rose sounded shocked. "I went into his room as usual. I took his shirts in for one thing. And of course I dusted the room. We dust all the rooms every day."

"Had the bed been slept in?"

She stared at him. "The bed, sir? Oh no."

"Was it rumpled—creased in any way?"

She shook her head.

"What about the bathroom?"

"There was a damp hand towel, sir, that had been used, I presume that would be the evening before. He may have washed his hands last thing before going off."

"And there was nothing to show that he had come back into the room—perhaps quite late—after midnight?"

She stared at him with an air of bewilderment. Father opened his mouth, then shut it again. Either she knew nothing about the canon's return or she was a highly accomplished actress.

"What about his clothes—suits. Were they packed up in his suitcases?"

"No, sir, they were hanging up in the cupboards. He was keeping his room on, you see, sir."

"Who did pack them up?"

"Miss Gorringe gave orders, sir. When the room was wanted for the new lady coming in."

A straightforward coherent account. But if that old lady was correct in stating that she saw Canon Pennyfather leaving his room at 3 A.M. on Friday morning, then he must have come back to that room sometime. Nobody had seen him enter the hotel. Had he, for some reason, deliberately avoided being seen? He had left no traces in the room. He hadn't even lain down on the bed. Had Miss Marple dreamed the whole thing? At her age it was possible enough. An idea struck him.

"What about his airport bag?"

"I beg your pardon, sir?"

"A small bag, dark blue—a B.E.A. or B.O.A.C. bag—you must have seen it?"

"Oh that—yes, sir. But of course he'd take that with him abroad."

"But he didn't go abroad. He never went to Switzerland after all. So he must have left it behind. Or else he came back and left it here with his other luggage."

"Yes—yes—I think—I'm quite sure—I believe he did."

Quite unsolicited, the thought raced into Father's mind: They didn't brief you on that, did they?

Rose Sheldon had been calm and competent up till now. But that question had rattled her. She hadn't known the right answer to it. But she ought to have known.

The canon had taken his bag to the airport, had been turned away from the airport. If he had come back to Bertram's, the bag would have been with him. But Miss Marple had made no mention of it when she had described the canon leaving his room and going down the stairs.

Presumably it was left in the bedroom, but it had not been put in the baggage room with the suitcases. Why not? Because the canon was supposed to have gone to Switzerland?

He thanked Rose genially and went downstairs again.

Canon Pennyfather! Something of an enigma, Canon Pennyfather. Talked a lot about going to Switzerland, muddled up things so that he didn't go to Switzerland, came back to his hotel so secretly that nobody saw him, left it again in the early hours of the morning. (To go where? To do what?)

Could absent-mindedness account for all this?

If not, then what was Canon Pennyfather up to? And more important, where was he?

From the staircase, Father cast a jaundiced eye over the occupants of the lounge, and wondered whether anyone was what they seemed to be. He had got to that stage! Elderly people, middle-aged people (nobody very young) nice old-fashioned people, nearly all well-to-do, all highly respectable. Service people, lawyers, clergymen, American husband and wife near the door, a French family near the fireplace. Nobody flashy, nobody out of place, most of them enjoying an old-fashioned English afternoon tea. Could there really be anything seriously wrong with a place that served old-fashioned afternoon teas?

The Frenchman made a remark to his wife that fitted in appositively enough.

"Le Five-o'-clock," he was saying. *"C'est bien Anglais ça, n'est-ce pas?"* He looked round him with approval.

Le Five o'clock, thought Davy as he passed through the swing doors to the street. That chap doesn't know that "le Five o'clock" is as dead as the dodo!

Outside, various vast American wardrobe cases and suitcases were being loaded on to a taxi. It seemed that Mr. and Mrs. Elmer Cabot were on their way to the Hotel Vendôme, Paris.

Beside him on the curb, Mrs. Elmer Cabot was expressing her views to her husband.

"The Pendleburys were quite right about this place, Elmer. It just is old England. So beautifully Edwardian. I just feel Edward the Seventh could walk right in any moment and sit down there for his afternoon tea. I mean to come back here next year—I really do."

"If we've got a million dollars or so to spare," said her husband dryly.

"Now, Elmer, it wasn't as bad as all that."

The baggage was loaded, the tall commissionaire

helped them in, murmuring "Thank you, sir" as Mr. Cabot made the expected gesture. The taxi drove off. The commissionaire transferred his attention to Father.

"Taxi, sir?"

Father looked up at him.

Over six feet. Good-looking chap. A bit run to seed. Ex-Army. Lot of medals—genuine, probably. A bit shifty? Drinks too much.

Aloud he said, "Ex-Army man?"

"Yes, sir. Irish Guards."

"Military Medal, I see. Where did you get that?"

"Burma."

"What's your name?"

"Michael Gorman. Sergeant."

"Good job here?"

"It's a peaceful spot."

"Wouldn't you prefer the Hilton?"

"I would not. I like it here. Nice people come here, and quite a lot of racing gentlemen—for Ascot and Newbury. I've had good tips from them now and. again."

"Ah, so you're an Irishman and gambler, is that it?"

"Och! now, what would life be without a gamble?"

"Peaceful and dull," said Chief Inspector Davy. "Like mine."

"Indeed, sir?"

"Can you guess what my profession is?" asked Father.

The Irishman grinned.

"No offense to you, sir, but if I may guess I'd say you were a cop."

"Right first time," said Chief Inspector Davy. "You remember Canon Pennyfather?"

"Canon Pennyfather now, I don't seem to mind the name—"

"Elderly clergyman."

Michael Gorman laughed.

"Ah now, clergymen are as thick as peas in a pod in there."

"This one disappeared from here."

"Oh, that one!" The commissionaire seemed slightly taken aback.

"Did you know him?"

"I wouldn't remember him if it hadn't been for people asking me questions about him. All I know is, I put him into a taxi and he went to the Athenaeum Club. That's the last I saw of him. Somebody told me he'd gone to Switzerland, but I hear he never got there. Lost himself, it seems."

"You didn't see him later that day?"

"Later—No, indeed."

"What time do you go off duty?"

"Eleven-thirty."

Chief Inspector Davy nodded, refused a taxi and moved slowly away along Pond Street. A car roared past him close to the curb, and pulled up outside Bertram's Hotel, with a scream of brakes. Chief Inspector Davy turned his head soberly and noted the number place. FAN 2266. There was something reminiscent about that number, though he couldn't for the moment place it.

Slowly he retraced his steps. He had barely reached the entrance before the driver of the car, who had gone through the door a moment or two before, came out again. He and the car matched each other. It was a racing model, white with long gleaming lines. The young man had the same eager greyhound look with a handsome face and a body with not a superfluous inch of flesh on it.

The commissionaire held the car door open, the young man jumped in, tossed a coin to the commissionaire and drove off with a burst of powerful engine.

"You know who he is?" said Michael Gorman to Father.

"A dangerous driver, anyway."

"Ladislaus Malinowski. Won the Grand Prix two years ago—world champion he was. Had a bad smash last year. They say he's all right again now."

"Don't tell me he's staying at Bertram's. Highly unsuitable."

Michael Gorman grinned.

"He's not staying here, no. But a friend of his is—" He winked.

A porter in a striped apron came out with more American luxury travel equipment.

Father stood absent-mindedly watching them being ensconced in a Daimler hire car while he tried to remember what he knew about Ladislaus Malinowski. A reckless fellow—said to be tied up with some well-known woman—what was her name now? Still staring at a smart wardrobe case, he was just turning away when he changed his mind and entered the hotel again.

He went to the desk and asked Miss Gorringe for the hotel register. Miss Gorringe was busy with departing Americans, and pushed the book along the counter towards him. He turned the pages. Lady Selina Hazy, Little Cottage, Merryfield, Hants. Mr. and Mrs. Hennessey King, Elderberries, Essex. Sir John Woodstock, 5 Beaumont Crescent, Cheltenham. Lady Sedgwick, Hurstings House, Northumberland. Mr. and Mrs.

Elmer Cabot, Greenwich, Connecticut. General Radley, 14, The Green, Chichester. Mr. and Mrs. Woolmer Pickington, Marblehead, Massachusetts. La Comtesse de Beauville, Les Sapins, St. Germain en Laye. Miss Jane Marple, St. Mary Mead, Much Benham. Colonel Luscombe, Little Green, Suffolk. Mrs. Carpenter, The Hon. Elvira Blake. Canon Pennyfather, The Close, Chadminster. Mrs. Holding, Miss Holding, Miss Audrey Holding, The Manor House, Carmanton. Mr. and Mrs. Ryesville, Valley Forge, Pennsylvania. The Duke of Barnstable, Doone Castle, N. Devon. . . . A cross section of the kind of people who stayed at Bertram's Hotel. They formed, he thought, a kind of pattern.

As he shut the book, a name on an earlier page caught his eye. Sir William Ludgrove.

Mr. Justice Ludgrove who had been recognized by a probation officer near the scene of a bank robbery. Mr. Justice Ludgrove—Canon Pennyfather—both patrons of Bertram's Hotel. . . .

"I hope you enjoyed your tea, sir?" It was Henry, standing at his elbow. He spoke courteously, and with the slight anxiety of the perfect host.

"The best tea I've had for years," said Chief Inspector Davy.

He remembered he hadn't paid for it. He attempted to do so; but Henry raised a deprecating hand.

"Oh no, sir. I was given to understand that your tea was on the house. Mr Humfries' orders."

Henry moved away. Father was left uncertain whether he ought to have offered Henry a tip or not. It was galling to think that Henry knew the answer to that social problem much better than he did.

As he moved away along the street, he stopped suddenly. He took out his notebook and put down a name and an address—no time to lose. He went into a telephone box. He was going to stick out his neck. Come hell or high water, he was going all out on a hunch.

16

It was the wardrobe that worried Canon Pennyfather. It worried him before he was quite awake. Then he forgot it and he fell asleep again. But when his eyes opened once more, there the wardrobe still was in the wrong place. He was lying on his left side facing the window and the wardrobe ought to have been there between him and the window on the left wall. But it wasn't. It was on the right. It worried him. It worried him so much that it made him feel tired. He was conscious of his head aching badly, and on top of that, to have the wardrobe in the wrong place. . . . At this point once more his eyes closed.

There was rather more light in the room the next time he woke. It was not daylight yet. Only the faint light of dawn. "Dear me," said Canon Pennyfather to himself, suddenly solving the problem of the wardrobe. "How stupid I am! Of course, I'm not at home."

He moved gingerly. No, this wasn't his own bed. He was away from home. He was—where was he? Oh, of course. He'd gone to London, hadn't he? He was in Bertram's Hotel and—but no, he wasn't in Bertram's Hotel. In Bertram's Hotel his bed was facing the window. So that was wrong, too.

"Dear me, where can I be?" said Canon Penny-father.

Then he remembered that he was going to Lucerne. "Of course," he said to himself, "I'm in Lucerne." He began thinking about the paper he was going to read. He didn't think about it long. Thinking about his paper seemed to make his head ache so he went to sleep again.

The next time he woke his head was a great deal clearer. Also there was a good deal more light in the room. He was not at home, he was not at Bertram's Hotel and he was fairly sure that he was not in Lucerne. This wasn't a hotel bedroom at all. He studied it fairly closely. It was an entirely strange room with very little furniture in it. A kind of cupboard (what he'd taken for the wardrobe) and a window with flowered curtains through which the light came. A chair and a table and a chest of drawers. Really, that was about all.

"Dear me," said Canon Pennyfather, "this is most odd. Where am I?"

He was thinking of getting up to investigate but when he sat up in bed his headache began again so he lay down.

"I must have been ill," decided Canon Pennyfather. "Yes, definitely I must have been ill." He thought a minute or two and then said to himself, "As a matter of fact, I think perhaps I'm still ill. Influenza, perhaps?" Influenza, people often said, came on very suddenly. Perhaps—perhaps it had come on at dinner at the Athenaeum. Yes that was right. He remembered that he had dined at the Athenaeum.

There were sounds of moving about in the house. Perhaps they'd taken him to a nursing home. But no, he didn't think this was a nursing home. With the increased light it showed itself as a rather shabby and ill-furnished small bedroom. Sounds of movement went on. From downstairs a voice called out, "Good-bye, ducks. Sausage and mash this evening."

Canon Pennyfather considered this. Sausage and mash. The words had a faintly agreeable quality.

"I believe," he said to himself, "I'm hungry."

The door opened. A middle-aged woman came in, went across to the curtains, pulled them back a little and turned towards the bed.

"Ah, you're awake now," she said. "And how are you feeling?"

"Really," said Canon Pennyfather, rather feebly, "I'm not quite sure."

"Ah, I expect not. You've been quite bad, you know. Something hit you a nasty crack, so the doctor said. These motorists! Not even stopping after they'd knocked you down."

"Have I had an accident?" said Canon Pennyfather. "A motor accident?"

"That's right," said the woman. "Found you by the side of the road when we come home. Thought you was drunk at first." She chuckled pleasantly at the reminiscence. "Then my husband said he'd better take a look. It may have been an accident, he said. There wasn't no smell of drink or anything. No blood or anything neither. Anyway, there you was, out like a log. So my husband said 'We can't leave him here lying like that' and he carried you in here. See?"

"Ah," said Canon Pennyfather, faintly, somewhat overcome by all these revelations. "A Good Samaritan."

"And he saw you were a clergyman so my husband said 'It's all quite respectable.' Then he said he'd better not call the police because being a clergyman and all that you mightn't like it. That's if you was drunk in spite of there being no smell of drink. So then we hit upon getting Dr. Stokes to come and have a look at you. We still call him Dr. Stokes although he's been struck off. A very nice man he is, embittered a bit, of course, by being struck off. It was only his kind heart really, helping a lot of girls who were no better than they should be. Anyway, he's a good enough doctor and we got him to come and take a look at you. He says you've come to no real harm, says it's mild concussion. All we'd got to do was to keep you lying flat and quiet in a dark room. 'Mind you,' he said, 'I'm not giving an opinion or anything like that. This is unofficial. I've no right to prescribe or to say anything. By rights I dare say you ought to report it to the police, but if you don't want to, why should you?' Give the poor old geezer a chance, that's what he said. Excuse me if I'm speaking disrespectful. He's a rough and ready speaker, the doctor is. Now what about a drop of soup and some hot bread and milk?"

"Either," said Canon Pennyfather faintly, "would be very welcome."

He relapsed on to his pillows. An accident? So that was it. An accident, and he couldn't remember a thing about it! A few minutes later the good woman returned bearing a tray with a steaming bowl on it.

"You'll feel better after this," she said. "I'd like to have put a drop of whisky or a drop of brandy in it but the doctor said you wasn't to have nothing like that."

"Certainly not," said Canon Pennyfather, "not with concussion. No. It would have been unadvisable."

"I'll put another pillow behind your back, shall I, ducks? There, is that all right?"

Canon Pennyfather was a little startled by being

155

addressed as "ducks." He told himself that it was kindly meant.

"Upsydaisy," said the woman, "there we are."

"Yes, but where are we?" said Canon Pennyfather. "I mean, where am I? Where is this place?"

"Milton St. John," said the woman. Didn't you know?"

"Milton St. John?" said Canon Pennyfather. He shook his head. "I never heard the name before."

"Oh well, it's not much of a place. Only a village."

"You have been very kind," said Canon Pennyfather. "May I ask your name?"

"Mrs. Wheeling. Emma Wheeling."

"You are most kind," said Canon Pennyfather again. "But this accient now. I simply cannot remember—"

"You put yourself outside that, luv, and you'll feel better and up to remembering things."

"Milton St. John," said Canon Pennyfather to himself, in a tone of wonder. "The name means nothing to me at all. How very extraordinary!"

17

Sir Ronald Graves drew a cat upon his blotting pad. He looked at the large portly figure of Chief Inspector Davy sitting opposite him and drew a bulldog.

"Ladislaus Malinowski?" he said. "Could be. Got any evidence?"

"No. He'd fit the bill, would he?"

"A daredevil. No nerves. Won the world championship. Bad crash about a year ago. Bad reputation with women. Sources of income doubtful. Spends money here and abroad very freely. Always going to and fro to the Continent. Have you got some idea that he's the man behind these big organized robberies and hold-ups?"

"I don't think he's the planner. But I think he's in with them."

"Why?"

"For one thing, he runs a Mercedes-Otto car. Racing model. A car answering to that description was seen near Bedhampton on the morning of the mail robbery. Different number plates—but we're used to that. And it's the same stunt—unlike, but not too unlike. FAN 2299 instead of 2266. There aren't so many Mercedes-

Otto models of that type about. Lady Sedgwick has one and young Lord Merrivale."

"You don't think Malinowski runs the show?

"No—I think there are better brains than his at the top. But he's in it. I've looked back over the files. Take the holdup at the Midland and West London. Three vans happened—just happened—to block a certain street. A Mercedes-Otto that was on the scene got clear away owing to that block."

"It was stopped later."

"Yes. And given a clean bill of health. Especially as the people who'd reported it weren't sure of the correct number. It was reported as FAM 3366—Malinowski's registration number is FAN 2266. It's all the same picture."

"And you persist in tying it up with Bertram's Hotel. They dug up some stuff about Bertram's for you—"

Father tapped his pocket. "Got it here. Properly registered company. Balance—paid up capital—directors—et cetera, et cetera. Doesn't mean a thing! These financial shows are all the same—just a lot of snakes swallowing each other. Companies, and holding companies—makes your brain reel."

"Come now, Father. That's just a way they have in the City. Has to do with taxation—"

"What I want is the real dope. If you'll give me a chit, sir, I'd like to go and see some top brass."

The A.C. stared at him. "And what exactly do you mean by top brass?"

Father mentioned a name.

The A.C. looked upset. "I don't know about that. I hardly think we dare approach *him*."

"It might be very helpful."

There was a pause. The two men looked at each

other. Father looked bovine, placid, and patient. Sir Ronald gave in.

"You're a stubborn old devil, Fred," he said. "Have it your own way. Go and worry the top brains behind the international financiers of Europe."

"He'll know," said Chief Inspector Davy. "He'll know. And if he doesn't, he can find out by pressing one buzzer on his desk or making one telephone call."

"I don't know that he'll be pleased."

"Probably not," said Father, "but it won't take much of his time. I've got to have authority behind me, though."

"You're really serious about this place, Bertram's aren't you? But what have you to go on? It's well run, has a good respectable clientele—no trouble with the licensing laws."

"I know—I know. No drinks, no drugs, no gambling, no accommodation for criminals. All pure as the driven snow. No beatniks, no thugs, no juvenile delinquents. Just sober Victorian-Edwardian old ladies, county families, visiting travellers from Boston and the more respectable parts of the U.S.A. All the same, a respectable canon of the church is seen to leave it at three A.M. in the morning in a somewhat surreptitious manner—"

"Who saw that?"

"An old lady."

"How did she manage to see him? Why wasn't she in bed and asleep?"

"Old ladies are like that, sir."

"You're not talking of—what's his name—Canon Pennyfather?"

"That's right, sir. His disappearance was reported and Campbell has been looking into it."

"Funny coincidence—his name's just come up in

connection with the mail robbery at Bedhampton."

"Indeed? In what way, sir?"

"Another old lay—or middle-aged anyway. When the train was stopped by that signal that had been tampered with, a good many people woke up and looked out into the corridor. This woman, who lives in Chadminster and knows Canon Pennyfather by sight, says she saw him entering the train by one of the doors. She thought he'd got out to see what was wrong and was getting in again. We were going to follow it up because of his disappearance being reported—"

"Let's see—the train was stopped at five-thirty A.M. Canon Pennyfather left Bertram's Hotel not long after three A.M. Yes, it could be done. If he were driven there—say—in a racing car. . . ."

"So we're back again to Ladislaus Malinowski!"

The A.C. looked at his blotting pad doodles. "What a bulldog you are, Fred," he said.

Half an hour later Chief Inspector Davy was entering a quiet and rather shabby office.

The large man behind the desk rose and put forward a hand.

"Chief Inspector Davy? Do sit down," he said. "Do you care for a cigar?"

Chief Inspector Davy shook his head.

"I must apologize," he said, in his deep countryman's voice, "for wasting your valuable time."

Mr. Robinson smiled. He was a fat man and very well dressed. He had a yellow face, his eyes were dark and sad-looking and his mouth was large and generous. He frequently smiled to display over-large teeth. "The better to eat you with," thought Chief Inspector Davy irrelevantly. His English was perfect and without accent but he was not an Englishman.

Father wondered, as many others had wondered before him, what nationality Mr. Robinson really was.

"Well, what can I do for you?"

"I'd like to know," said Chief Inspector Davy, "who owns Bertram's hotel."

The expression on Mr. Robinson's face did not change. He showed no surprise at hearing the name nor did he show recognition. He said thoughtfully:

"You want to know who owns Bertram's Hotel. That, I think, is in Pond Street, off Piccadilly."

"Quite right, sir."

"I have occasionally stayed there myself. A quiet place. Well run."

"Yes," said Father, "particularly well run."

"And you want to know who owns it? Surely that is easy to ascertain?"

There was a faint irony behind his smile.

"Through the usual channels, you mean? Oh yes." Father took a small piece of paper from his pocket and read out three or four names and addresses.

"I see," said Mr. Robinson, "someone has taken quite a lot of trouble. Interesting. And you come to me?"

"If anyone knows, you would, sir."

"Actually I do not know. But it is true that I have ways of obtaining information. One has"—he shrugged his very large, fat shoulders—"one has contacts."

"Yes, sir," said Father with an impassive face.

Mr. Robinson looked at him, then he picked up the telephone on his deck.

"Sonia? Get me Carlos," He waited a minute or two then spoke again. "Carlos?" He spoke rapidly half a dozen sentences in a foreign language. It was not a language that Father could even recognize.

Father could converse in good British French. He had a smattering of Italian and he could make a guess at plain travellers' German. He knew the sounds of Spanish, Russian and Arabic, though he could not understand them. This language was none of those. At a faint guess he hazarded it might be Turkish or Persian or Armenian, but even of that he was by no means sure. Mr. Robinson replaced the receiver.

"I do not think," he said genially, "that we shall have long to wait. I am interested, you know. Very much interested. I have occasionally wondered my-self—"

Father looked inquiring.

"About Bertram's Hotel," said Mr. Robinson. "Financially, you know. One wonders how it can pay. However, it had never been any of my business. And one appreciates"—he shrugged his shoulders—"a comfortable hostelry with an unusually talented per-sonnel and staff. Yes, I have wondered." He looked at Father. "You know how and why?"

"Not yet," said Father, "but I mean to."

"There are several possibilities," said Mr. Robinson, thoughtfully. "It is like music, you know. Only so many notes to the octave, yet one can combine them in—what is it—several million different ways? A musician told me once that you do not get the same tune twice. Most interesting."

There was a slight buzz on his desk and he picked up the receiver once more.

"Yes? Yes, you have been very prompt. I am pleased. I see. Oh! Amsterdam, yes. . . . Ah. . . . Thank you . . . Yes. You will spell that? Good."

He wrote rapidly on a pad at his elbow.

"I hope this will be useful to you," he said, as he tore off the sheet and passed it across the table to

Father, who read the name out loud. "Wilhelm Hoffman."

"Nationality Swiss," said Mr. Robinson. "Though not, I would say, born in Switzerland. Has a good deal of influence in banking circles and though keeping strictly on the right side of the law, he has been behind a great many—questionable deals. He operates solely on the Continent, not in this country."

"Oh."

"But he has a brother," said Mr. Robinson. "Robert Hoffman. Living in London—a diamond merchant—most respectable business. His wife is Dutch. He also has offices in Amsterdam. Your people may know about him. As I say, he deals mainly in diamonds, but he is a very rich man, and he owns a lot of property, not usually in his own name. Yes, he is behind quite a lot of enterprises. He and his brother are the real owners of Bertram's Hotel."

"Thank you, sir." Chief Inspector Davy rose to his feet. "I needn't tell you that I'm much obliged to you. It's wonderful," he added, allowing himself to show more enthusiasm than was normal.

"That I should know?" inquired Mr. Robinson, giving one of his larger smiles. "But that is one of my specialities. Information. I like to know. That is why you came to me, is it not?"

"Well," said Chief Inspector Davy, "we do know about you. The Home Office. The Special Branch and all the rest of it." He added almost naïvely, "It took a bit of nerve on my part to approach you."

Again Mr. Robinson smiled. "I find you an interesting personality, Chief Inspector Davy," he said. "I wish you success in whatever you are undertaking."

"Thank you, sir. I think I shall need it. By the way,

these two brothers, would you say they were violent men?"

"Certainly not," said Mr. Robinson. "It would be quite against their policy. The brothers Hoffman do not apply violence in business matters. They have other methods that serve them better. Year by year, I would say, they get steadily richer, or so my information from Swiss banking circles tells me."

"It's a useful place, Switzerland," said Chief Inspector Davy.

"Yes, indeed. What we should all do without it I do not know! So much rectitude. Such a fine business sense! Yes, we businessmen must all be very grateful to Switzerland. I myself," he added, "have also a high opinion of Amsterdam." He looked hard at Davy, then smiled again, and the Chief Inspector left.

When he got back to headquarters again, he found a note awaiting him.

Canon Pennyfather has turned up—safe if not sound. Apparently was knocked down by a car at Milton St. John and has concussion.

18

Canon Pennyfather looked at Chief Inspector Davy and Inspector Campbell, and Chief Inspector Davy and Inspector Campbell looked at him. Canon Pennyfather was at home again. Sitting in the big armchair in his library, a pillow behind his head and his feet up on a pouffe, with a rug over his knees to emphasize his invalid status.

"I'm afraid," he was saying politely, "that I simply cannot remember anything at all."

"You can't remember the accident when the car hit you?"

"I'm really afraid not."

"Then how did you know a car did hit you?" demanded Inspector Campbell acutely.

"The woman there, Mrs.—Mrs.—was her name Wheeling?—told me about it."

"And how did she know?"

Canon Pennyfather looked puzzled.

"Dear me, you are quite right. She couldn't have known, could she? I suppose she thought it was what must have happened."

"And you really cannot remember anything? How did you come to be in Milton St. John?"

"I've no idea," said Canon Pennyfather. "Even the name is quite unfamiliar to me."

Inspector Campbell's exasperation was mounting, But Chief Inspector Davy said in his soothing, homely voice:

"Just tell us again the last thing you do remember, sir."

Canon Pennyfather turned to him with relief. The inspector's dry skepticism had made him uncomfortable.

"I was going to Lucerne to a congress. I took a taxi to the airport—at least to Kensington Air Station."

"Yes. And then?"

"That's all. I can't remember any more. The next thing I remember is the wardrobe."

"What wardrobe?" demanded Inspector Campbell.

"It was in the wrong place."

Inspector Campbell was tempted to go into this question of a wardrobe in the wrong place. Chief Inspector Davy cut in.

"Do you remember arriving at the air station, sir?"

I suppose so," said Canon Pennyfather, with the air of one who has a great deal of doubt on the matter.

"And you duly flew to Lucerne."

"Did I? I don't remember anything about it if so."

"Do you remember arriving back at Bertram's Hotel that night?"

"No."

"You do remember Bertram's Hotel?"

"Of course. I was staying there. Very comfortable. I kept my room on."

"Do you remember travelling in a train?"

"A train? No, I can't recall a train."

"There was a hold-up. The train was robbed. Surely, Canon Pennyfather, you can remember that."

"I ought to, oughtn't I?" said Canon Pennyfather. "But somehow"—he spoke apologetically—"I don't." He looked from one to the other of the officers with a bland gentle smile.

"Then your story is that you remember nothing after going in a taxi to the air station until you woke up in the Wheelings' cottage at Milton St. John."

"There is nothing unusual in that," the Canon assured him. "It happens quite often in cases of concussion."

"What did you think had happened to you when you woke up?"

"I had such a headache I really couldn't think. Then of course I began to wonder where I was and Mrs. Wheeling explained and brought me some excellent soup. She called me 'love' and 'dearie,' and 'ducks,'" said the canon with slight distaste, "but she was very kind. Very kind indeed."

"She ought to have reported the accident to the police. Then you would have been taken to hospital and properly looked after," said Campbell.

"She looked after me very well," the canon protested, with spirit, "and I understand that with concussion there is very little you can do except keep the patient quiet."

"If you should remember anything more, Canon Pennyfather—"

The canon interrupted him.

"Four whole days I seem to have lost out of my life," he said. "Very curious. Really very curious indeed. I wonder so much where I was and what I was doing. The doctor tells me it may all come back to me. On the other hand it may not. Possibly I shall never know what happened to me during those days." His eyelids flickered. "You'll excuse me. I think I am rather tired."

"That's quite enough now," said Mrs. McCrae, who had been hovering by the door, ready to intervene if she thought it necessary. She advanced upon them. "Doctor says he wasn't to be worried," she said firmly.

The policeman rose and moved towards the door. Mrs. McCrae shepherded them out into the hall rather in the manner of a conscientious sheepdog. The canon murmured something and Chief Inspector Davy who was the last to pass through the door wheeled round at once.

"What was that?" he asked, but the canon's eyes were now closed.

"What did you think he said?" said Campbell as they left the house after refusing Mrs. McCrae's lukewarm offer of refreshment.

Father said thoughtfully, "I thought he said 'the walls of Jericho.'"

"What could he mean by that?"

"It sounds Biblical," said Father.

"Do you think we'll ever know," asked Campbell, "how that old boy got from the Cromwell Road to Milton St. John?"

"It doesn't seem as if we shall get much help from him," agreed Davy.

"That woman who says she saw him on the train after the holdup. Can she possibly be right? Can he be mixed up in some way with these robberies? It seems impossible. He's such a thoroughly respectable old boy. Can't very well suspect a canon of Chadminster Cathedral of being mixed up with a train robbery, can one?"

"No," said Father thoughtfully, "no. No more than

one can imagine Mr. Justice Ludgrove being mixed up with a bank holdup."

Inspector Campbell looked at his superior officer curiously.

The expedition to Chadminster concluded with a short and unprofitable interview with Dr. Stokes.

Dr. Stokes was aggressive, un-co-operative and rude.

"I've known the Wheelings quite a while. They're by way of being neighbours of mine. They'd picked some old chap up off the road. Didn't know whether he was dead drunk, or ill. Asked me in to have a look. I told them he wasn't drunk—that it was conscussion—"

"And you treated him for that."

"Not at all. I didn't treat him, or prescribe for him or attend him. I'm not a doctor—I was once, but I'm not now—I told them what they ought to do was ring up the police. Whether they did or not I don't know. Not my business. They're a bit dumb, both of them—but kindly folk."

"You didn't think of ringing up the police yourself?"

"No, I did not. I'm not a doctor. Nothing to do with me. As a human being I told them not to pour whisky down his throat and to keep him quiet and flat until the police came."

He glared at them and, reluctantly, they had to leave it at that.

19

Mr. Hoffman was a big solid-looking man. He gave the appearance of being carved out of wood—preferably teak.

His face was so expressionless as to give rise to surmise—could such a man be capable of thinking, of feeling emotion? It seemed impossible.

His manner was highly correct.

He rose, bowed, and held out a wedgelike hand. "Chief Inspector Davy? It is some years since I had the pleasure—you may not even remember—"

"Oh yes, I do, Mr. Hoffman. The Aaronberg diamond case. You were a witness for the Crown—a most excellent witness, let me say. The Defense was quite unable to shake you."

"I am not easily shaken," said Mr. Hoffman gravely.

He did not look a man who would easily be shaken.

"What can I do for you?" he went on. "No trouble, I hope—I always want to agree well with the police. I have the greatest admiration for your superb police force."

"Oh, there is no trouble. It is just that we wanted you to confirm a little information."

"I shall be delighted to help you in any way I can.

As I say, I have the highest opinion of your London police force. You have such a splendid class of men. So full of integrity, so fair, so just."

"You'll make me embarrassed," said Father.

"I am at your service. What is it that you want to know?"

"I was just going to ask you to give me a little dope about Bertram's Hotel."

Mr. Hoffman's face did not change. It was possible that his entire attitude became for a moment or two even more static than it had been before—that was all.

"Bertram's Hotel?" he said. His voice was inquiring, slightly puzzled. It might have been that he had never heard of Bertram's Hotel or that he could not quite remember whether he knew Bertram's Hotel or not.

"You have a connection with it, have you not, Mr. Hoffman?"

Mr. Hoffman moved his shoulders. "There are so many things," he said. "One cannot remember them all. So much business, so much—it keeps me very busy."

"You have your fingers in a lot of pies, I know that."

"Yes." Mr. Hoffman smiled a wooden smile. "I pull out many plums, that is what you think? And so you believe I have a connection with this—Bertram's Hotel?"

"I shouldn't have said a connection. As a matter of fact, you own it, don't you?" said Father genially.

This time, Mr. Hoffman definitely did stiffen. "Now who told you that, I wonder?" he said softly.

"Well, it's true, isn't it?" said Chief Inspector Davy cheerfully. "Very nice place to own, I should say. In fact, you must be quite proud of it."

"Oh yes," said Hoffman. "For the moment—I could not quite remember—you see"—he smiled deprecatingly—"I own quite a lot of property in London. It is a good investment—property. If something comes on the market in what I think is a good position, and there is a chance of snapping it up cheap, I invest."

"And was Bertram's Hotel going cheap?"

"As a running concern, it had gone down the hill," said Mr. Hoffman, shaking his head.

"Well, it's on its feet now," said Father. "I was in there just the other day. I was very much struck with the atmosphere there. Nice old-fashioned clientele, comfortable old-fashioned premises, nothing rackety about it, a lot of luxury without looking luxurious."

"I know very little about it personally," explained Mr. Hoffman. "It is just one of my investments—but I believe it is doing well."

"Yes, you seem to have a first-class fellow running it. What is his name? Humfries? Yes, Humfries."

"An excellent man," said Mr. Hoffman. "I leave everything to him. I look at the balance sheet once a year to see that all is well."

"The place was thick with titles," said Father. "Rich travelling Americans, too." He shook his head thoughtfully. "Wonderful combination."

"You say you were in there the other day?" Mr. Hoffman inquired. "Not—not officially, I hope?"

"Nothing serious. Just trying to clear up a little mystery."

"A mystery? In Bertram's Hotel?"

"So it seems. The Case of the Disappearing Clergyman, you might label it."

"That is a joke," Mr. Hoffman said. "That is your Sherlock Holmes language."

"This clergyman walked out of the place one evening and was never seen again."

"Peculiar," said Mr. Hoffman, "but such things

happen. I remember many, many years ago now, a great sensation. Colonel—now let me think of his name—Colonel Fergusson I think, one of the equerries of Queen Mary. He walked out of his club one night and he, too, was never seen again."

"Of course," said Father, with a sigh, "a lot of these disappearances are voluntary."

"You know more about that than I do, my dear Chief Inspector," said Mr. Hoffman. He added, "I hope they gave you every assistance at Bertram's Hotel?"

"They couldn't have been nicer," Father assured him. "That Miss Gorringe, she has been with you some time, I believe?"

"Possibly. I really know so very little about it. I take no personal interest, you understand. In fact—" he smiled disarmingly, "I was surprised that you even knew it belonged to me."

It was not quite a question; but once more there was a slight uneasiness in his eyes. Father noted it without seeming to.

"The ramifications that go on in the City are like a gigantic jigsaw," he said. "It would make my head ache if I had to deal with that side of things. I gather that a company—Mayfair Holding Trust or some name like that—is the registered owner. They're owned by another company and so on and so on. The real truth of the matter is that it belongs to you. Simple as that. I'm right, aren't I?"

"I and my fellow directors are what I dare say you'd call behind it, yes," admitted Mr. Hoffman rather reluctantly.

"Your fellow directors. And who might they be? Yourself and, I believe, a brother of yours?"

"My brother Wilhelm is associated with me in this

venture. You must understand that Bertram's is only a part of a chain of various hotels, offices, clubs, and other London properties."

"Any other directors?"

"Lord Pomfret, Abel Isaacstein." Hoffman's voice was suddenly edged. "Do you really need to know all these things? Just because you are looking into the Case of the Disappearing Clergyman?"

Father shook his head and looked apologetic. "I suppose it's really curiosity. Looking for my disappearing clergyman was what took me to Bertram's, but then I got—well, interested if you understand what I mean. One thing leads to another sometimes, doesn't it?"

"I suppose that could be so, yes. And now," he smiled, "your curiosity is satisfied?"

"Nothing like coming to the horse's mouth when you want information, is there?" said Father genially. He rose to his feet. "There's only one thing I'd really like to know—and I don't suppose you'll tell me that."

"Yes, Chief Inspector?" Hoffman's voice was wary.

"Where do Bertram's get hold of their staff? Wonderful! That fellow what's-his-name—Henry. The one that looks like an archduke or an archbishop, I'm not sure which. Anyway, he serves you tea and muffins— most wonderful muffins! An unforgettable experience."

"You like muffins with much butter, yes?" Mr. Hoffman's eyes rested for a moment on the rotundity of Father's figure with disapprobation.

"I expect you can see I do," said Father. "Well, I mustn't be keeping you. I expect you're pretty busy taking over take-over bids, or something like that."

"Ah. It amuses you to pretend to be ignorant of all these things. No, I am not busy. I do not let business absorb me too much. My tastes are simple. I live simply, with leisure, with growing of roses, and my family to whom I am much devoted."

"Sounds ideal," said Father. "Wish I could live like that."

Mr. Hoffman smiled and rose ponderously to shake hands with him.

"I hope you will find your disappearing clergyman very soon."

"Oh! that's all right. I'm sorry I didn't make myself clear. He's found—disappointing case, really. Had a car accident and got concussion—simple as that."

Father went to the door, then turned. "By the way, is Lady Sedgwick a director of your company?" he asked.

"Lady Sedgwick?" Hoffman took a moment or two. "No. Why should she be?"

"Oh well, one hears things. Just a shareholder?"

"I—yes."

"Well, good-bye, Mr. Hoffman. Thanks very much."

Father went back to the Yard and straight to the Assistant Commissioner.

"The two Hoffman brothers are the ones behind Bertram's Hotel—financially."

"What? Those scoundrels?" demanded Sir Ronald. "Yes."

"They've kept it very dark."

"Yes—and Robert Hoffman didn't half like our finding it out. It was a shock to him."

"What did he say?"

"Oh, we kept it all very formal and polite. He tried, not too obviously, to learn how I found out about it."

"And you didn't oblige him with that information, I suppose."

"I certainly did not."

"What excuse did you give for going to see him?"

"I didn't give any," said Father.

"Didn't he think that a bit odd?"

"I expect he did. On the whole I thought that was a good way to play it, sir."

"If the Hoffmans are behind all this, it accounts for a lot. They're never concerned in anything crooked themselves—oh no! They don't organize crime—they finance it though!

"Wilhelm deals with the banking side from Switzerland. He was behind those foreign currency rackets just after the war. We knew it, but we couldn't prove it. Those two brothers control a great deal of money and they use it for backing all kinds of enterprises—some legitimate, some not. But they're careful—they know every trick of the trade. Robert's diamond broking is straightforward enough, but it makes a suggestive picture—diamonds, banking interests, and property—clubs, cultural foundations, office buildings, restaurants, hotels—all apparently owned by somebody else."

"Do you think Hoffman is the planner of these organized robberies?"

"No, I think those two deal only with finance. No, you'll have to look elsewhere for your planner. Somewhere there's a first-class brain at work."

20

The fog had come down over London suddenly that evening. Chief Inspector Davy pulled up his coat collar and turned into Pond Street. Walking slowly like a man who was thinking of something else, he did not look particularly purposeful but anyone who knew him well would realize that his mind was wholly alert. He was prowling as a cat prowls before the moment comes for it to pounce on its prey.

Pond Street was quiet tonight. There were few cars about. The fog had been patchy to begin with, had almost cleared, then had deepened again. The noise of the traffic from Park Lane was muted to the level of a suburban side road. Most of the buses had given up. Only from time to time individual cars went on their way with determined optimism. Chief Inspector Davy turned up a cul-de-sac, went to the end of it and came back again. He turned again, aimlessly as it seemed, first one way, then the other, but he was not aimless. Actually his cat prowl was taking him in a circle round one particular building. Bertram's Hotel. He was appraising carefully just what lay to the east of it, to the west of it, to the north of it and to the south of it. He examined the cars that were parked by the pavement, he examined the cars that were in the cul-de-sac. He examined a mews with special care. One car in particular interested him and he stopped. He pursed up his lips and said softly, "So you're here again, you beauty." He checked the number and nodded to himself. "FAN 2266 tonight, are you?" He bent down and ran his fingers over the number plate delicately, then nodded approval. "Good job they made of it," he said under his breath.

He went on, came out at the other end of the mews, turned right and right again and came out in Pond Street once more, fifty yards from the entrance of Bertram's Hotel. Once again he paused, admiring the handsome lines of yet another racing car.

"You're a beauty, too," said Chief Inspector Davy. "Your number plate's the same as the last time I saw you. I rather fancy your number plate always is the same. And that should mean"—he broke off—"or should it?" he muttered. He looked up towards what could have been the sky. "Fog's getting thicker," he said to himself.

Outside the door to Bertram's, the Irish commissionaire was standing swinging his arms backwards and forwards with some violence to keep himself warm. Chief Inspector Davy said good evening to him.

"Good evening, sir. Nasty night."

"Yes. I shouldn't think anyone would want to go out tonight who hadn't got to."

The swing doors were pushed open and a middle-aged lady came out and paused uncertainly on the step.

"Want a taxi, ma'am?"

"Oh dear. I meant to walk."

"I wouldn't if I were you, ma'am. It's very nasty, this fog. Even in a taxi it won't be too easy."

"Do you think you could find me a taxi?" asked the lady doubtfully.

"I'll do my best. You go inside now, and keep warm and I'll come in and tell you if I've got one." His voice changed, modulated to a persuasive tone. "Unless you have to, ma'am, I wouldn't go out tonight at all."

"Oh dear. Perhaps you're right. But I'm expected at some friends in Chelsea. I don't know. It might be very difficult getting back here. What do you think?"

Michael Gorman took charge.

"If I were you, ma'am," he said firmly, "I'd go in and telephone to your friends. It's not nice for a lady like you to be out on a foggy night like this."

"Well—really—yes, well, perhaps you're right."

She went back in again.

"I have to look after them," said Micky Gorman turning in an explanatory manner to Father. "That kind would get her bag snatched, she would. Going out this time of night in a fog and wandering about Chelsea or West Kensington or wherever she's trying to go."

"I suppose you've had a good deal of experience of dealing with elderly ladies?" said Davy.

"Ah yes, indeed. This place is a home from home to them, bless their aging hearts. How about you, sir. Were you wanting a taxi?"

"Don't suppose you could get me one if I did," said Father. "There don't seem to be many about in this. And I don't blame them."

"Ah, now, I might lay my hand on one for you. There's a place round the corner where there's usually a taxi driver got his cab parked, having a warm up and a drop of something to keep the cold out."

"A taxi's no good to me," said Father with a sigh.

He jerked his thumb towards Bertram's Hotel. "I've got to go inside. I've got a job to do."

"Indeed now? Would it be still the missing canon?"

"Not exactly. He's been found."

"Found?" The man stared at him. "Found where?"

"Wandering about with concussion after an accident."

"Ah, that's just what one might expect of him. Crossed the road without looking, I expect."

"That seems to be the idea," said Father.

He nodded, and pushed through the doors into the hotel. There were not very many people in the lounge this evening. He saw Miss Marple sitting in a chair near the fire and Miss Marple saw him. She made, however, no sign of recognition. He went towards the desk. Miss Gorringe, as usual, was behind her books. She was, he thought, faintly discomposed to see him. It was a very slight reaction, but he noted the fact.

"You remember me, Miss Gorringe," he said. "I came here the other day."

"Yes, of course I remember you, Chief Inspector. Is there anything more you want to know? Do you want to see Mr. Humfries?"

"No thank you. I don't think that'll be necessary. I'd just like one more look at your register if I may."

"Of course." She pushed it along to him.

He opened it and looked slowly down the pages. To Miss Gorringe he gave the appearance of a man looking for one particular entry. In actuality this was not the case. Father had an accomplishment which he had learned early in life and had developed into a highly-skilled art. He could remember names and addresses with a perfect and photographic memory. That memory would remain with him for twenty-four or even forty-eight hours. He shook his head as he shut the book and returned it to her.

"Canon Pennyfather hasn't been in, I suppose?" he said in a light voice.

"Canon Pennyfather?"

"You know he's turned up again?"

"No indeed. Nobody has told me. Where?"

"Some place in the country. Car accident it seems. Wasn't reported to us. Some good Samaritan just picked him up and looked after him."

"Oh, I am pleased. Yes, I really am very pleased. I was worried about him."

"So were his friends," said Father. "Actually I was looking to see if one of them might be staying here now. Archdeacon—Archdeacon—I can't remember his name now, but I'd know it if I saw it."

"Tomlinson?" said Miss Gorringe helpfully. "He is due next week. From Salisbury."

"No, not Tomlinson. Well, it doesn't matter." He turned away.

It was quiet in the lounge tonight.

An ascetic-looking middle-aged man was reading through a badly typed thesis, occasionally writing a comment in the margin in such small crabbed handwriting as to be almost illegible. Every time he did this, he smiled in vinegary satisfaction.

There weer one or two married couples of long standing who had little need to talk to each other. Occasionally two or three people were gathered together in the name of the weather conditions, discussing anxiously how they or their families were going to get where they wanted to be.

"—I rang up and begged Susan not to come by car . . . it means the M. One and always so dangerous in fog—"

"They say it's clearer in the Midlands. . . ."

Chief Inspector Davy noted them as he passed. Without haste, and with no seeming purpose, he arrived at his objective.

Miss Marple was sitting near the fire and observing his approach.

"So you're still here, Miss Marple. I'm glad."

"I go tomorrow," said Miss Marple.

That fact had, somehow, been implicit in her attitude. She had sat, not relaxed, but upright, as one sits in an airport lounge, or a railway waiting room. Her luggage, he was sure, would be packed, only toilet things and night wear to be added.

"It is the end of my fortnight's holiday," she explained.

"You've enjoyed it, I hope?"

Miss Marple did not answer at once. "In a way—yes . . ." She stopped.

"And in another way, no?"

"It's difficult to explain what I mean—"

"Aren't you, perhaps, a little too near the fire? Rather hot, here. Wouldn't you like to move—into that corner perhaps."

Miss Marple looked at the corner indicated, then she looked at Chief Inspector Davy. "I think you are quite right," she said.

He gave her a hand up, carried her handbag and her book for her and established her in the quiet corner he had indicated.

"All right?"

"Quite all right."

"You know why I suggested it?"

"You thought—very kindly—that it was too hot for me by the fire. Besides," she added, "our conversation cannot be overheard here."

"Have you got something you want to tell me, Miss Marple?"

"Now why should you think that?"

"You looked as though you had," said Davy.

"I'm sorry I showed it so plainly," said Miss Marple. "I didn't mean to."

"Well, what about it?"

"I don't know if I ought to do so. I would like you to believe, Inspector, that I am not really fond of interfering. I am against interference. Though often well meant, it can cause a great deal of harm."

"It's like that, is it? I see. Yes, it's quite a problem for you."

"Sometimes one sees people doing things that seem to one unwise—even dangerous. But has one any right to interfere? Usually not, I think."

"Is this Canon Pennyfather you're talking about?"

"Canon Pennyfather?" Miss Marple sounded very surprised. "Oh no. Oh dear me, no, nothing whatever to do with him. It concerns—a girl."

"A girl, indeed? And you thought I could help?"

"I don't know," said Miss Marple. "I simply don't know. But I'm worried, very worried."

Father did not press her. He sat there looking large and comfortable and rather stupid. He let her take her time. She had been willing to do her best to help him, and he was quite prepared to do anything he could to help her. He was not, perhaps, particularly interested. On the other hand, one never knew.

"One reads in the papers," said Miss Marple in a low clear voice, "accounts of proceedings in court; of young people, children or girls 'in need of care and protection.' It's just a sort of legal phrase, I suppose, but it could mean something real."

"This girl you mentioned, you feel she is in need of care and protection?"

"Yes. Yes, I do."

"Alone in the world?"

"Oh no," said Miss Marple. "Very much not so, if I may put it that way. She is to all outward appearances very heavily protected and very well cared for."

"Sounds interesting," said Father.

"She was staying in this hotel," said Miss Marple, "with a Mrs. Carpenter, I think. I looked in the register to see the name. The girl's name is Elvira Blake."

Father looked up with a quick air of interest.

"She was a lovely girl. Very young, very much as I say, sheltered and protected. Her guardian was a Colonel Luscombe, a very nice man. Quite charming. Elderly, of course, and I am afraid terribly innocent."

"The guardian or the girl?"

"I meant the guardian," said Miss Marple. "I don't know about the girl. But I do think she is in danger. I came across her quite by chance in Battersea Park. She was sitting at a refreshment place there with a young man."

"Oh, that's it, is it?" said Father. "Undesirable, I suppose. Beatnik—spiv—thug—"

"A very handsome man," said Miss Marple. "Not so very young. Thirty-odd, the kind of man that I should say is very attractive to women, but his face is a bad face. Cruel, hawklike, predatory."

"He mayn't be as bad as he looks," said Father soothingly.

"If anything he is worse than he looks," said Miss Marple. "I am convinced of it. He drives a large racing car."

Father looked up quickly. "Racing car?"

"Yes. Once or twice I've seen it standing near this hotel."

"You don't remember the number, do you?"

"Yes, indeed I do. FAN 2266. I had a cousin who stuttered," Miss Marple explained. "That's how I remember it."

Father looked puzzled.

"Do you know who he is?" demanded Miss Marple.

"As a matter of fact I do," said Father slowly. "Half French, half Polish. Very well-known racing driver, he was world champion three years ago. His name is Ladislaus Malinowski. You're quite right in some of your views about him. He has a bad reputation where women are concerned. That is to say, he is not a suitable friend for a young girl. But it's not easy to do anything about that sort of thing. I suppose she is meeting him on the sly, is that it?"

"Almost certainly," said Miss Marple.

"Did you approach her guardian?"

"I don't know him," said Miss Marple. "I've only just been introduced to him once by a mutual friend. I don't like the idea of going to him in a tale-bearing way. I wondered if perhaps in some way you could do something about it."

"I can try," said Father. "By the way, I thought you might like to know that your friend Canon Pennyfather has turned up all right."

"Indeed!" Miss Marple looked animated. "Where?"

"A place called Milton St. John."

"How every odd. What was he doing there? Did he know?"

"Apparently"—Chief Inspector Davy stressed the word—"he had had an accident."

"What kind of an accident?"

"Knocked down by a car—concussed—or else, of course, he might have been conked on the head."

"Oh, I see." Miss Marple considered the point. "Doesn't he know himself?"

"He *says*"—again the Chief Inspector stressed the word—"that he does not know anything."

"Very remarkable."

"Isn't it? The last thing he remembers is driving in a taxi to Kensington Air Station."

Miss Marple shook her head perplexedly.

"I know it does happen that way in concussion," she murmured. "Didn't he say anything—useful?"

"He murmured something about the walls of Jericho."

"Joshua?" hazarded Miss Marple, "or archaeology—excavations?—or I remember, long ago, a play—by Mr. Sutro, I think."

"And all this week north of the Thames, Gaumont Cinemas—*The Walls of Jericho,* featuring Olga Radbourne and Bart Levinne," said Father.

Miss Marple looked at him suspiciously.

"He could have gone to that film in the Cromwell Road. He could have come out about eleven and come back here—though if so, someone ought to have seen him—it would be well before midnight—"

"Took the wrong bus," Miss Marple suggested. "Something like that—"

"Say he got back here after midnight," Father said. "He could have walked up to his room without anyone seeing him. But if so, what happened then—and why did he go out again three hours later?"

Miss Marple groped for a word. "The only idea that occurs to me is—oh!"

She jumped as a report sounded from the street outside.

"Car backfiring," said Father soothingly.

"I'm sorry to be so jumpy. I am nervous tonight—that feeling one has—"

"That something's going to happen? I don't think you need worry."

"I have never liked fog."

"I wanted to tell you," said Chief Inspector Davy, "that you've given me a lot of help. The things you've noticed here—just little things—they've added up."

"So there was something wrong with this place?"

"There was and is everything wrong with it."

Miss Marple sighed. "It seemed wonderful at first—unchanged you know—like stepping back into the past —to the part of the past that one had loved and enjoyed."

She paused. "But of course, it wasn't really like that, I learned (what I suppose I really knew already) that one can never go back, that one should not ever try to go back—that the essence of life is going forward. Life is really a one way street, isn't it?"

"Something of the sort," agreed Father.

"I remember," said Miss Marple, diverging from her main topic in a characteristic way, "I remember being in Paris with my mother and my grandmother, and we went to have tea at the Elysée Hotel. And my grandmother looked round, and she said suddenly, 'Clara, I do believe I am the only woman here in a bonnet!' And she was, too! When she got home she packed up all her bonnets and her beaded mantles, too, and sent them off—"

"To the jumble sale?" inquired Father sympathetically.

"Oh no. Nobody would have wanted them at a jumble sale. She sent them to a theatrical repertory company. They appreciated them very much. But let me see—" Miss Marple recovered her direction. "Where was I?"

"Summing up this place."

"Yes. It seemed all right, but it wasn't. It was mixed up—real people and people who weren't real. One couldn't always tell them apart."

"What do you mean by not real?"

"There were retired military men, but there were also what seemed to be military men but who had never been in the Army. And clergymen who weren't clergymen. And admirals and sea captains who've never been in the Navy. My friend Selina Hazy—it amused me at first how she was always so anxious to recognize people she knew (quite natural, of course) and how often she was mistaken and they weren't the people she thought they were. But it happened too often. And so—I began to wonder. Even Rose, the chambermaid—so nice—but I began to think that perhaps she wasn't real, either."

"If it interests you to know, she's an ex-actress. A good one. Gets a better salary here than she ever drew on the stage."

"But—why?"

"Mainly, as part of the décor. Perhaps there's more than that to it."

"I'm glad to be leaving here," said Miss Marple. She gave a little shiver. "Before anything happens."

Chief Inspector Davy looked at her curiously.

"What do you expect to happen?" he asked.

"Evil of some kind," said Miss Marple.

"Evil is rather a big word—"

"You think it is too melodramatic? But I have some experience. I seem to have been—so often—in contact with murder."

"Murder?" Chief Inspector Davy shook his head.

"I'm not suspecting murder. Just a nice cozy roundup of some remarkably clever criminals—"

"That's not the same thing. Murder—the wish to do murder—is something quite different. It—how shall I say?—it defies God."

He looked at her and shook his head gently and reassuringly.

"There won't be any murders," he said.

A sharp report, louder than the former one, came from outside. It was followed by a scream and another report.

Chief Inspector Davy was on his feet, moving with a speed surprising in such a bulky man. In a few seconds he was through the swing doors and out in the street.

II

The screaming—a woman's—was piercing the mist with a note of terror. Chief Inspector Davy raced down Pond Street in the direction of the screams. He could dimly visualize a woman's figure backed against a railing. In a dozen strides he had reached her. She wore a long pale fur coat, and her shining blonde hair hung down each side of her face. He thought for a moment that he knew who she was, then he realized that this was only a slip of a girl. Sprawled on the pavement at her feet was the body of a man in uniform. Chief Inspector Davy recognized him. It was Michael Gorman.

As Davy came up to the girl, she clutched at him, shivering all over, stammering out broken phrases.

"Someone tried to kill me. . . . Someone . . . they shot at me. . . . If it hadn't been for him—" She pointed down at the motionless figure at her feet.

"He pushed me back and got in front of me—and then the second shot came . . . and he fell. . . . He saved my life. I think he's hurt—badly hurt. . . ."

Chief Inspector Davy went down on one knee. His torch came out. The tall Irish commissionaire had fallen like a soldier. The left-hand side of his tunic showed a wet patch that was growing wetter as the blood oozed out into the cloth. Davy rolled up an eyelid, touched a wrist. He rose to his feet again.

"He's had it all right," he said.

The girl gave a sharp cry. "Do you mean he's *dead?* Oh no, no! He can't be *dead.*"

"Who was it shot at you?"

"I don't know. . . . I'd left my car just round the corner and was feeling my way along by the railings —I was going to Bertram's Hotel. And then suddenly there was a shot—and a bullet went past my cheek and then—he—the doorman from Bertram's—came running down the street towards me, and shoved me behind him, and then another shot came. . . . I think —I think whoever it was must have been hiding in that area there."

Chief Inspector Davy looked where she pointed. At this end of Bertram's Hotel there was an old-fashioned area below the level of the street, with a gate and some steps down to it. Since it gave only on some store rooms it was not much used. But a man could have hidden there easily enough.

"You didn't see him?"

"Not properly. He rushed past me like a shadow. It was all thick fog."

Davy nodded.

The girl began to sob hysterically.

"But who could possibly want to kill me? Why

should anyone want to kill me? That's the second time. I don't understand. . . . Why?"

One arm round the girl, Chief Inspector Davy fumbled in his pocket with the other hand.

The shrill notes of a police whistle penetrated the mist.

III

In the lounge of Bertram's Hotel, Miss Gorringe had looked up sharply from the desk.

One or two of the visitors had looked up also. The older and deafer did not look up.

Henry, about to lower a glass of old brandy to a table, stopped poised with it still in his hand.

Miss Marple sat forward, clutching the arms of her chair.

"Accident!" a retired admiral said decisively. "Cars collided in the fog, I expect."

The swing doors from the street were pushed open. Through them came what seemed like an outsize policeman, looking a good deal larger than life.

He was supporting a girl in a pale fur coat. She seemed hardly able to walk. The policeman looked round for help with some embarrassment.

Miss Gorringe came out from behind the desk, prepared to cope. But at that moment the elevator came down. A tall figure emerged, and the girl shook herself free from the policeman's support, and ran frantically across the lounge.

"Mother," she cried. "Oh Mother, Mother. . . ." and threw herself, sobbing, into Bess Sedgwick's arms.

21

Chief Inspector Davy settled himself back in his chair and looked at the two women sitting opposite him. It was past midnight. Police officials had come and gone. There had been doctors, fingerprint men, an ambulance to removed the body; and now everything had narrowed to this one room dedicated for the purposes of the Law by Bertram's Hotel. Chief Inspector Davy sat one side of the table. Bess Sedgwick and Elvira sat the other side. Against the wall a policeman sat unobtrusively writing. Detective Sergeant Wadell sat near the door.

Father looked thoughtfully at the two women facing him. Mother and daughter. There was, he noted, a strong superficial likeness between them. He could understand how for one moment in the fog he had taken Elvira Blake for Bess Sedgwick. But now, looking at them, he was more struck by the points of difference than the points of resemblance. They were not really alike save in colouring, yet the impression persisted that here he had a positive and a negative version of the same personality. Everything about Bess Sedgwick was positive. Her vitality, her energy, her magnetic attraction. He admired Lady Sedgwick. He always had admired her. He had admired her courage and had always been excited over her exploits; had said, reading his Sunday papers: "She'll never get away with that," and invariably she had got away with it! He had not thought it possible that she would reach journey's end and she had reached journey's end. He admired particularly the indestructible quality of her. She had had one air crash, several car crashes, had been thrown badly twice from her horse, but at the end of it here she was. Vibrant, alive, a personality one could not ignore for a moment. He took off his hat to her mentally. Some day, of course, she would come a cropper. You could only bear a charmed life for so long. His eyes went from mother to daughter. He wondered. He wondered very much.

In Elvira Blake, he thought, everything had been driven inward. Bess Sedgwick had got through life by imposing her will on it. Elvira, he guessed, had a different way of getting through life. She submitted, he thought. She obeyed. She smiled in compliance and behind that, he thought, she slipped away through your fingers. "Sly," he said to himself, appraising that fact. "That's the only way she can manage, I expect. She can never brazen things out or impose herself. That's why, I expect, the people who've looked after her have never had the least idea of what she might be up to."

He wondered what she had been doing slipping along the street to Bertram's Hotel on a late foggy evening. He was going to ask her presently. He thought it highly probable that the answer he would get would not be the true one. That's the way, he thought, that the poor child defends herself. Had she come here to meet her mother or to find her mother? It was perfectly possible, but he didn't think so. Not for a moment. Instead he thought of the big sports car tucked away round the corner—the car with the number plate FAN 2266. Ladislaus Malinowski must be somewhere in the neighbourhood since his car was there.

"Well," said Father, addressing Elvira in his most kindly and fatherlike manner, "well, and how are you feeling now?"

"I'm quite all right," said Elvira.

"Good. I'd like you to answer a few questions if you feel up to it; because, you see, time is usually the essence of these things. You were shot at twice and a man was killed. We want as many clues as we can get to the person who killed him."

"I'll tell you everything I can, but it all came so suddenly. And you can't see anything in a fog. I've no idea myself who it could have been—or even what he looked like. That's what was so frightening."

"You said this was the second time somebody had tried to kill you. Does that mean there was an attempt on your life before?"

"Did I say that? I can't remember." Her eyes moved uneasily. "I don't think I said that."

"Oh, but you did, you know," said Father.

"I expect I was just being—being hysterical."

"No," said Father, "I don't think you were. I think you meant just what you said."

"I might have been imagining things," said Elvira. Her eyes shifted again.

Bess Sedgwick moved. "You'd better tell him, Elvira," she said quietly.

Elvira shot a quick, uneasy look at her mother.

"You needn't worry," said Father reassuringly.

"We know quite well in the police force that girls don't tell their mothers or their guardians everything.

We don't take those things too seriously, but we've got to know about them, because, you see, it all helps."

"Was it in Italy?" Bess Sedgwick said.

"Yes," said Elvira.

Father said, "That's where you've been at school, isn't it, or to a finishing place or whatever they call it nowadays?"

"Yes. I was at Contessa Martinelli's. There were about eighteen or twenty of us."

"And you thought that somebody tried to kill you. How was that?"

"Well, a big box of chocolates and sweets and things came for me. There was a card with it written in Italian in a flowery hand. The sort of thing they say, you know, 'To the bellissima Signorina.' Something like that. And my friends and I—well, we laughed about it a bit, and wondered who'd sent it."

"Did it come by post?"

"No. No, it couldn't have come by post. It was just there in my room. Someone must have put it there."

"I see. Bribed one of the servants, I suppose. I am to take it that you didn't let the Contessa whoever-it-was in on this?"

A faint smile appeared on Elvira's face. "No. No. We certainly didn't. Anyway we opened the box and they were lovely chocolates. Different kinds, you know, but there were some violet creams. That's the sort of chocolate that has a crystallized violet on top. My favourite. So of course I ate one or two of those first. And then afterwards, in the night, I felt terribly ill. I didn't think it was the chocolates, I just thought it was something perhaps that I'd eaten at dinner."

"Anybody else ill?"

"No. Only me. Well, I was very sick and all that, but I felt all right by the end of the next day. Then a day or two later I ate another of the same chocolates, and the same thing happened. So I talked to Bridget about it. Bridget was my special friend. And we looked at the chocolates, and we found that the violet creams had got a sort of hole in the bottom that had been filled up again, so we thought that someone had put some poison in and they'd only put it in the violet creams so that I would be the one who ate them."

"Nobody else was ill?"

"No."

"So presumably nobody else ate the violet creams?"

"No. I don't think they could have. You see, it was my present and they knew I liked the violet ones, so they'd leave them for me."

"The chap took a risk, whoever he was," said Father. "The whole place might have been poisoned."

"It's absurd," said Lady Sedgwick sharply. "Utterly absurd! I never heard of anything so crude."

Chief Inspector Davy made a slight gesture with his hand. "Please," he said, then he went on to Elvira. "Now I find that very interesting, Miss Blake. And you still didn't tell the Contessa?"

"Oh no, we didn't. She'd have made a terrible fuss."

"What did you do with the chocolates?"

"We threw them away," said Elvira. "They were lovely chocolates," she added, with a tone of slight grief.

"You didn't try and find out who sent them?"

Elvira looked embarrassed. "Well, you see, I thought it might have been Guido."

"Yes?" said Chief Inspector Davy cheerfully. "And who is Guido?"

"Oh, Guido. . . ." Elvira paused. She looked at her mother.

"Don't be stupid," said Bess Sedgwick. "Tell Chief

Inspector Davy about Guido, whoever he is. Every girl of your age has a Guido in her life. You met him out there, I suppose?"

"Yes. When we were taken to the opera. He spoke to me there. He was nice. Very attractive. I used to see him sometimes when we went to classes. He used to pass me notes."

"And I suppose," said Bess Sedgwick, "that you told a lot of lies, and made plans with some friends and you managed to get out and meet him? Is that it?"

Elvira looked relieved by this short cut to confession. "Yes. Bridget and I sometimes went out together. Sometimes Guido managed to—"

"What was Guido's other name?"

"I don't know," said Elvira. "He never told me."

Chief Inspector Davy smiled at her. "You mean you're not going to tell? Never mind. I dare say we'll be able to find out quite all right without your help, if it should really matter. But why should you think that this young man who was presumably fond of you, should want to kill you?"

"Oh, because he used to threaten things like that. I mean, we used to have rows now and then. He'd bring some of his friends with him, and I'd pretend to like them better than him, and then he'd get very, very wild and angry. He said I'd better be careful what I did. I couldn't give him up just like that! That if I wasn't faithful to him he'd kill me! I just thought he was being melodramatic and theatrical." Elvira smiled suddenly and unexpectedly. "But it was all rather fun. I didn't think it was real or serious."

"Well," said Chief Inspector Davy, "I don't think it does seem very likely that a young man such as you describe would really poison chocolates and send them to you."

"Well, I don't think so really either," said Elvira, "but it must have been him because I can't see that there's anyone else. It worried me. And then, when I came back here, I got a note—" She stopped.

"What sort of a note?"

"It just came in an envelope and was printed. It said: *Be on your guard. Somebody wants to kill you.*"

Chief Inspector Davy's eyebrows went up. "Indeed? Very curious. Yes, very curious. And it worried you. You were frightened?"

"Yes. I began to—to wonder who could possibly want me out of the way. That's why I tried to find out if I was really very rich."

"Go on."

"And the other day in London something else happened. I was in the tube and there were a lot of people on the platform. I thought someone tried to push me onto the track."

"My dear child!" said Bess Sedgwick. "Don't romance."

Again Father made the slight gesture of his hand.

"Yes," said Elvira apologetically. "I expect I have been imagining it all but—I don't know—I mean, after what happened this evening it seems, doesn't it, as though it might all be true?" She turned suddenly to Bess Sedgwick, speaking with urgency, "Mother! You might know. Does anyone want to kill me? Could there be anyone? Have I got an enemy?"

"Of course you've not got an enemy," said Bess Sedgwick impatiently. "Don't be an idiot. Nobody wants to kill you. Why should they?"

"Then who shot at me tonight?"

"In that fog," said Bess Sedgwick, "you might have

been mistaken for someone else. That's possible, don't you think?" she said, turning to Father.

"Yes, I think it might be quite possible," said Chief Inspector Davy.

Bess Sedgwick was looking at him very intently. He almost fancied the motion of her lips saying "later."

"Well," he said cheerfully, "we'd better get down to some more facts now. Where had you come from tonight? What were you doing walking along Pond Street on such a foggy evening?"

"I came up for an art class at the Tate this morning. Then I went to lunch with my friend Bridget. She lives in Onslow Square. We went to a film and when we came out, there was this fog—quite thick and getting worse, and I thought perhaps I'd better not drive home."

"You drive a car, do you?"

"Yes. I took my driving test last summer. Only, I'm not a very good driver and I hate driving in fog. So Bridget's mother said I could stay the night, so I rang up Cousin Mildred—that's where I live in Kent—"

Father nodded.

"—and I said I was going to stay up overnight. She said that was very wise."

"And what happened next?" asked Father.

"And then the fog seemed lighter suddenly. You know how patchy fogs are. So I said I would drive down to Kent after all. I said good-bye to Bridget and started off. But then it began to come down again. I didn't like it very much. I ran into a very thick patch of it and I lost my way and I didn't know where I was. Then after a bit I realized I was at Hyde Park Corner and I thought: I really can't go down to Kent in this. At first, I thought I'd go back to Bridget's but then I remembered how I'd lost my way already. And then I realized that I was quite close to this nice hotel where Uncle Derek took me, when I came back from Italy and I thought: I'll go there and I'm sure they can find me a room. That was fairly easy, I found a place to leave the car and then I walked back up the street towards the hotel."

"Did you meet anyone or did you hear anyone walking near you?"

"It's funny you saying that, because I did think I heard someone walking behind me. Of course, there must be lots of people walking about in London. Only in a fog like this, it gives you a nervous feeling. I waited and listened but I didn't hear any footsteps and I thought I'd imagined them. I was quite close to the hotel by then."

"And then?"

"And then quite suddenly there was a shot. As I told you, it seemed to go right past my ear. The commissionaire man who stands outside the hotel came running down towards me and he pushed me behind him and then—then—the other shot came. . . . He— he fell down and I screamed." She was shaking now. Her mother spoke to her.

"Steady, girl," said Bess in a low, firm voice. "Steady now." It was the voice Bess Sedgwick used for her horses and it was quite as efficacious when used on her daughter. Elvira blinked at her, drew herself up a little, and became calm again.

"Good girl," said Bess.

"And then you came," said Elvira to Father. "You blew your whistle, you told the policeman to take me into the hotel. And as soon as I got in, I saw—I saw Mother." She turned and looked at Bess Sedgwick.

"And that brings us more or less up to date," said Father. He shifted his bulk a little in the chair.

"Do you know a man called Ladislaus Malinowski?" he asked. His tone was even, casual, without any direct inflection. He did not look at the girl, but he was aware, since his ears were functioning at full attention, of a quick little gasp she gave. His eyes were not on the daughter but on the mother.

"No," said Elvira, having waited just a shade too long to say it. "No, I don't."

"Oh," said Father. "I thought you might. I thought he might have been here this evening."

"Oh? Why should he be here this evening."

"Well, his car is here," said Father. "That's why I thought he might be."

"I don't know him," said Elvira.

"My mistake," said Father. "You do, of course?" he turned his head towards Bess Sedgwick.

"Naturally," said Bess Sedgwick. "Known him for many years." She added, smiling slightly, "He's a madman, you know. Drives like an angel or a devil—he'll break his neck one of these days. Had a bad smash eighteen months ago."

"Yes, I remember reading about it," said Father. "Not racing again yet, is he?"

"No, not yet. Perhaps he never will."

"Do you think I could go to bed now?" asked Elvira, plaintively. "I'm—really terribly tired."

"Of course. You must be," said Father. "You've told us all you can remember?"

"Oh, yes."

"I'll go up with you," said Bess.

Mother and daughter went out together.

"She knows him all right," said Father.

"Do you really think so?" asked Sergeant Wadell.

"I know it. She had tea with him in Battersea Park only a day or two ago."

"How did you find that out?"

"Old lady told me—distressed. Didn't think he was a nice friend for a young girl. He isn't, of course."

"Especially if he and the mother—" Wadell broke off delicately. "It's pretty general gossip—"

"Yes. May be true, may not. Probably is."

"In that case which one is he really after?"

Father ignored that point. "I want him picked up. I want him badly," he said. "His car's here—just round the corner."

"Do you think he might be actually staying in this hotel?"

"Don't think so. It wouldn't fit into the picture. He's not supposed to be here. If he came here, he came to meet the girl. She definitely came to meet him, I'd say."

The door opened and Bess Sedgwick reappeared.

"I came back," she said, "because I wanted to speak to you." She looked from him to the other two men. "I wonder if I could speak to you alone? I've given you all the information I have, such as it is; but I would like a word or two with you in private."

"I don't see any reason why not," said Chief Inspector Davy. He motioned with his head, and the young detective constable took his notebook and went out. Wadell went with him. "Well?" said Chief Inspector Davy.

Lady Sedgwick sat down again opposite him.

"That silly story about poisoned chocolates," she said. "It's nonsense. Absolutely ridiculous. I don't believe anything of the kind ever happened."

"You don't, eh?"

"Do you?"

Father shook his head doubtfully. "You think your daughter cooked it up?"

"Yes. But why?"

"Well, if you don't know why," said Chief Inspector Davy, "how should I know? She's your daughter. Presumably you know her better than I do."

"I don't know her at all," said Bess Sedgwick bitterly. "I've not seen her or had anything to do with her since she was two years old, when I ran away from my husband."

"Oh yes. I know all that. I find it curious. You see, Lady Sedgwick, courts usually give the mother, even if she is a guilty party in a divorce, custody of a young child if she asks for it. Presumably then you didn't ask for it? You didn't want it."

"I thought it—better not."

"Why?"

"I didn't think it was—safe for her."

"On moral grounds?"

"No. Not on moral grounds. Plenty of adultery nowadays. Children have to learn about it, have to grow up with it. No. It's just that I am not really a safe person to be with. The life I'd lead wouldn't be a safe life. You can't help the way you're born. I was born to live dangerously. I'm not law-abiding or conventional. I thought it would be better for Elvira, happier, to have a proper English conventional bringing-up. Shielded, looked after. . . ."

"But minus a mother's love?"

"I thought if she learned to love me it might bring sorrow to her. Oh, you mayn't believe me, but that's what I felt."

"I see. Do you still think you were right?"

"No," said Bess. "I don't. I think now I may have been entirely wrong."

"Does your daughter know Ladislaus Malinowski?"

"I'm sure she doesn't. She said so. You heard her."

"I heard her, yes."

"Well, then?"

"She was afraid, you know, when she was sitting here. In our profession we get to know fear when we meet up with it. She was afraid—why? Chocolates or no chocolates, her life has been attempted. That tube story may be true enough—"

"It was ridiculous. Like a thriller—"

"Perhaps. But that sort of thing does happen, Lady Sedgwick. Oftener than you'd think. Can you give me any idea who might want to kill your daughter?"

"Nobody—nobody at all!"

She spoke vehemently.

Chief Inspector Davy sighed and shook his head.

22

Chief Inspector Davy waited patiently until Mrs. Melford had finished talking. It had been a singularly unprofitable interview. Cousin Mildred had been incoherent, unbelieving and generally feather-headed. Or that was Father's private view. Accounts of Elvira's sweet manners, nice nature, troubles with her teeth, odd excuses told through the telephone, had led on to serious doubts whether Elvira's friend Bridget was really a suitable friend for her. All these matters had been presented to the Chief Inspector in a kind of general hasty pudding. Mrs. Melford knew nothing, had heard nothing, had seen nothing and had apparently deduced very little.

A short telephone call to Elvira's guardian Colonel Luscombe had been even more unproductive, though fortunately less wordy. "More Chinese monkeys," he muttered to his sergeant as he put down the receiver. "See no evil, hear no evil, speak no evil.

"The trouble is that everyone who's had anything to do with this girl has been far too nice—if you get my meaning. Too many nice people who don't know anything about evil. Not like my old lady."

"The Bertram's Hotel one?"

"Yes, that's the one. She's had a long life of experience in noticing evil, fancying evil, suspecting evil and going forth to do battle with evil. Let's see what we can get out of girl friend Bridget."

The difficulties in this interview were represented first, last, and most of the time by Bridget's mamma. To talk to Bridget without the assistance of her mother took all Chief Inspector Davy's adroitness and cajolery. He was, it must be admitted, ably seconded by Bridget. After a certain amount of stereo-typed questions and answers and expressions of horror on the part of Bridget's mother at hearing of Elvira's narrow escape from death, Bridget said, "You know it's time for that committee meeting, Mum. You said it was very important."

"Oh dear, dear," said Bridget's mother.

"You know they'll get into a frightful mess without you, Mummy."

"Oh, they will, they certainly will. But perhaps I ought—"

"Now that's quite all right, madam," said Chief Inspector Davy, putting on his kindly old father look. "You don't want to worry. Just you get off. I've finished all the important things. You've told me really everything I wanted to know. I've just one or two routine inquiries about people in Italy which I think your daughter Miss Bridget might be able to help me with."

"Well, if you think you could manage, Bridget—"

"Oh, I can manage, Mummy," said Bridget.

Finally, with a great deal of fuss, Bridget's mother went off to her committee.

"Oh dear," said Bridget, sighing, as she came back after closing the front door. "Really! I do think mothers are difficult."

"So they tell me," said Chief Inspector Davy. "A

lot of young ladies I come across have a lot of trouble with their mothers."

"I'd have thought you'd put it the other way round," said Bridget.

"Oh, I do, I do," said Davy. "But that's not how the young ladies see it. Now you can tell me a little more."

"I couldn't really speak frankly in front of Mummy," explained Bridget. "But I do feel, of course, that it is really important that you should know as much as possible about all this. I do know Elvira was terribly worried about something and afraid. She wouldn't exactly admit she was in danger, but she was."

"I thought that might have been so. Of course I didn't like to ask you too much in front of your mother."

"Oh no," said Bridget, "we don't want Mummy to hear about it. She gets in such a frightful state about things and she'd go and tell everyone. I mean, if Elvira doesn't want things like this to be known. . . ."

"First of all," said Chief Inspector Davy, "I want to know about a box of chocolates in Italy. I gather there was some idea that a box was sent to her which might have been poisoned."

Bridget's eyes opened wide. "Poisoned," she said. "Oh no. I don't think so. At least. . . ."

"There was something?"

"Oh yes. A box of chocolates came and Elvira did eat a lot of them and she was rather sick that night. Quite ill."

"But she didn't suspect poison?"

"No. At least—oh yes, she did say that someone was trying to poison one of us and we looked at the chocolates to see, you know, if anything had been injected into them."

"And had it?"

"No, it hadn't," said Bridget. "At least, not as far as we could see."

"But perhaps your friend, Miss Elvira, might still have thought so?"

"Well, she might—but she didn't say any more."

"But you think she was afraid of someone?"

"I didn't think so at the time or notice anything. It was only here, later."

"What about his man, Guido?"

Bridget giggled. "He had a terrific crush on Elvira," she said.

"And you and your friend used to meet him places?"

"Well, I don't mind telling you," said Bridget. "After all you're the police. It isn't important to you, that sort of thing and I expect you understand. Countess Martinelli was frightfully strict—or thought she was. And of course we had all sorts of dodges and things. We all stood in with each other. You know."

"And told the right lies, I suppose?"

"Well, I'm afraid so," said Bridget. "But what can one do when anyone is so suspicious?"

"So you did meet Guido and all that. And used he to threaten Elvira?"

"Oh, not seriously, I don't think."

"Then perhaps there was someone else she used to meet?"

"Oh—that—well, I don't know."

"Please tell me, Miss Bridget. It might be—vital, you know."

"Yes. Yes I can see that. Well there was someone. I don't know who it was, but there was someone else —she really minded about. She was deadly serious. I mean it was a really important thing."

"She used to meet him?"

"I think so. I mean she'd say she was meeting Guido but it wasn't always Guido. It was this other man."

"Any idea who it was?"

"No." Bridget sounded a little uncertain.

"It wouldn't be a racing motorist called Ladislaus Malinowski?"

Bridget gaped at him. "So you *know?*"

"Am I right?"

"Yes—I think so. She'd got a photograph of him torn out of a paper. She kept it under her stockings."

"That might have been just a pin-up hero, mightn't it?"

"Well it might, of course, but I don't think it was."

"Did she meet him here in this country, do you know?"

"I don't know. You see I don't really know what she's been doing since she came back from Italy."

"She came up to London to the dentist," Davy prompted her. "Or so she said. Instead she came to you. She rang up Mrs. Melford with some story about an old governess."

A faint giggle came from Bridget.

"That wasn't true, was it?" said the Chief Inspector smiling. "Where did she really go?"

Bridget hesitated and then said, "She went to Ireland."

"She went to Ireland, did she? Why?"

"She wouldn't tell me. She said there was something she had to find out."

"Do you know where she went in Ireland?"

"Not exactly. She mentioned a name. Bally something. Bally-gowlan, I think it was."

"I see. You're sure she went to Ireland?"

"I saw her off at Kensington Airport. She went by Aer Lingus."

"She came back when?"

"The following day."

"Also by air?"

"Yes."

"You're quite sure, are you, that she came back by air?"

"Well—I suppose she did!"

"Had she taken a return ticket?"

"No. No, she didn't. I remember."

"She might have come back another way, mightn't she?"

"Yes, I suppose so."

"She might have come back for instance by the Irish Mail?"

"She didn't say she had."

"But she didn't *say* she'd come by air, did she?"

"No," Bridget agreed. "But why should she come back by boat and train instead of by air?"

"Well, if she had found out what she wanted to know and had had nowhere to stay, she might think it would be easier to come back by the Irish Mail."

"Why, I suppose she might."

Davy smiled faintly.

"I don't suppose you young ladies," he said, "think of going anywhere except in terms of flying, do you, nowadays?"

"I suppose we don't really," agreed Bridget.

"Anyway, she came back to England. Then what happened? Did she come to you or ring you up?"

"She rang up."

"What time of day."

"Oh, in the morning some time. Yes, it must have been about eleven or twelve o'clock, I think."

"And she said, what?"

"Well, she just asked if everything was all right."

"And was it?"

"No, it wasn't, because, you see, Mrs. Melford had rung up and Mummy had answered the phone and things had been very difficult and I hadn't known what to say. So Elvira said she would not come to Onslow Square, but that she'd ring up her cousin Mildred and try to fix up some story or other."

"And that's all that you can remember?"

"That's all," said Bridget, making certain reservations. She thought of Mr. Bollard and the bracelet. That was certainly a thing she was not going to tell Chief Inspector Davy.

Father knew quite well that something was being kept from him. He could only hope that it was not something pertinent to his inquiry. He asked again: "You think your friend was really frightened of someone or something?"

"Yes I do."

"Did she mention it to you or did you mention it to her?"

"Oh, I asked her outright. At first she said no and then she admitted that she was frightened. And I know she was," went on Bridget violently. "She was in danger. She was quite sure of it. But I don't know why or how or anything about it."

"Your surety on this point relates to that particular morning, does it, the morning she had come back from Ireland?"

"Yes. Yes, that's when I was so sure about it."

"On the morning when she might have come back on the Irish Mail?"

"I don't think it's very likely that she did. Why don't you ask her?"

"I probably shall do in the end. But I don't want to call attention to that point. Not at the moment. It might just possibly make things more dangerous for her."

Bridget opened round eyes. "What do you mean?"

"You may not remember it, Miss Bridget, but that was the night, or rather the early morning, of the Irish Mail robbery."

"Do you mean that Elvira was in *that* and never told me a thing about it?"

"I agree it's unlikely," said Father. "But it just occurred to me that she might have seen something or someone, or some incident might have occurred connected with the Irish Mail. She might have seen someone she knew, for instance, and that might have put her in danger."

"Oh!" said Bridget. She thought it over. "You mean—someone she knew was mixed up in the robbery."

Chief Inspector Davy got up. "I think that's all," he said. "Sure there's nothing more you can tell me? Nowhere where your friend went that day? Or the day before?"

Again visions of Mr. Bollard and the Bond Street shop rose before Bridget's eyes.

"No," she said.

"I think there is something you haven't told me," said Chief Inspector Davy.

Bridget grasped thankfully at a straw. "Oh, I forgot," she said. "Yes. I mean she did go to some lawyers. Lawyers who were trustees, to find out something."

"Oh, she went to some lawyers who were her trustees. I don't suppose you know their name?"

"Their name was Egerton—Forbes, Egerton and

Something," said Bridget. "Lots of names. I think that's more or less right."

"I see. And she wanted to find out something, did she?"

"She wanted to know how much money she'd got," said Bridget.

Inspector Davy's eyebrows rose. "Indeed!" he said. "Interesting. Why didn't she know herself?"

"Oh, because people never told her anything about money," said Bridget. "They seem to think it's bad for you to know actually how much money you have."

"And she wanted to know badly, did she?"

"Yes," said Bridget. "I think she thought it was important."

"Well, thank you," said Chief Inspector Davy. "You've helped me a good deal."

23

Richard Egerton looked again at the official card in front of him, then up into the Chief Inspector's face.

"Curious business," he said.

"Yes, sir," said Chief Inspector Davy, "a very curious business."

"Bertram's Hotel," said Egerton, "in the fog. Yes it was a bad fog last night. I suppose you get a lot of that sort of thing in fogs, don't you? Snatch and grab—handbags—that sort of thing?"

"It wasn't quite like that," said Father. "Nobody attempted to snatch anything from Miss Blake."

"Where did the shot come from?"

"Owing to the fog we can't be sure. She wasn't sure herself. But we think—it seems the best idea—that the man may have been standing in the area."

"He shot at her twice, you say?"

"Yes. The first shot missed. The commissionaire rushed along from where he was standing outside the hotel door and shoved her behind him just before the second shot."

"So that he got hit instead, eh?"

"Yes."

"Quite a brave chap."

"Yes. He was brave," said the Chief Inspector. "His military record was very good. An Irishman."

"What's his name?"

"Gorman. Michael Gorman."

"Michael Gorman." Egerton frowned for a minute. "No," he said. "For a moment I thought the name meant something."

"It's a very common name, of course. Anyway, he saved the girl's life."

"And why exactly have you come to me, Chief Inspector?"

"I hoped for a little information. We always like full information, you know, about the victim of a murderous assault."

"Oh naturally, naturally. But really, I've only seen Elvira twice since she was a child."

"You saw her when she came to call upon you about a week ago, didn't you?"

"Yes, that's quite right. What exactly do you want to know? If it's anything about her personally, who her friends were or about boy friends, or lovers' quarrels —all that sort of thing—you'd do better to go to one of the women. There's a Mrs. Carpenter who brought her back from Italy, I believe, and there's Mrs. Melford with whom she lives in Sussex."

"I've seen Mrs. Melford."

"Oh."

"No good. Absolutely no good at all, sir. And I don't so much want to know about the girl personally —after all, I've seen her for myself and I've heard what she can tell me—or rather what she's willing to tell me—"

At a quick movement of Egerton's eyebrows he saw that the other had appreciated the point of the word "willing."

"I've been told that she was worried, upset, afraid about something, and convinced that her life was in danger. Was that your impression when she came to see you?"

"No," said Egerton, slowly, "no, I wouldn't go as far as that; though she did say one or two things that struck me as curious."

"Such as?"

"Well, she wanted to know who would benefit if she were to die suddenly."

"Ah," said Chief Inspector Davy, "so she had that possibility in her mind, did she? That she might die suddenly. Interesting."

"She'd got something in her head but I didn't know what it was. She also wanted to know how much money she had—or would have when she was twenty-one. That, perhaps, is more understandable."

"It's a lot of money I believe."

"It's a very large fortune, Chief Inspector."

"Why do you think she wanted to know?"

"About the money?"

"Yes, and about who would inherit it?"

"I don't know," said Egerton. "I don't know at all. She also brought up the subject of marriage—"

"Did you form the impression that there was a man in the case?"

"I've no evidence—but—yes, I did think just that. I felt sure there was a boy friend somewhere in the offing. There usually is! Luscombe—that's Colonel Luscombe, her guardian—doesn't seem to know anything about a boy friend. But then dear old Derek Luscombe wouldn't. He was quite upset when I suggested that there was such a thing in the background and probably an unsuitable one at that."

"He is unsuitable," said Chief Inspector Davy.

"Oh, then you know who he is?"

"I can have a very good guess at it. Ladislaus Malinowski."

"The racing motorist? Really! A handsome daredevil. Women fall for him easily. I wonder how he came across Elvira. I don't see very well where their orbits would meet except—yes, I believe he was in Rome a couple of months ago. Possibly she met him there."

"Very possibly. Or could she have met him through her mother?"

"What, through Bess? I wouldn't say that was at all likely."

Davy coughed. "Lady Sedgwick and Malinowski are said to be close friends, sir."

"Oh yes, yes, I know that's the gossip. May be true, may not. They are close friends—thrown together constantly by their way of life. Bess has had her affairs, of course; though, mind you, she's not the nymphomaniac type. People are ready enough to say that about a woman, but it's not true in Bess's case. Anyway, as far as I know, Bess and her daughter are practically not even acquainted with each other."

"That's what Lady Sedgwick told me. And you agree?"

Egerton nodded.

"What other relatives has Miss Blake got?"

"For all intents and purposes, none. Her mother's two brothers were killed in the war—and she was old Coniston's only child. Mrs. Melford, though the girl calls her 'Cousin Mildred,' is actually a cousin of Colonel Luscombe's. Luscombe's done his best for the girl in his conscientious old-fashioned way—but it's difficult . . . for a man."

"Miss Blake brought up the subject of marriage, you

217

say? There's no possibility, I suppose, that she may actually already be married—"

"She's well under age—she'd have to have the assent of her guardian and trustees."

"Technically, yes. But they don't always wait for that," said Father.

"I know. Most regrettable. One has to go through all the machinery of making them Wards of Court, and all the rest of it. And even that has its difficulties."

"And once they're married, they're married," said Father. "I suppose, if she were married, and died suddenly, her husband would inherit?"

"This idea of marriage is most unlikely. She has been most carefully looked after and . . ." He stopped, reacting to Chief Inspector Davy's cynical smile.

However carefully Elvira had been looked after, she seemed to have succeeded in making the acquaintance of the highly unsuitable Ladislaus Malinowski.

He said dubiously, "Her mother bolted, it's true."

"Her mother bolted, yes—that's what she would do —but Miss Blake's a different type. She's just as set on getting her own way, but she'd go about it differently."

"You don't really think—"

"I don't think anything—yet," said Chief Inspector Davy.

24

Ladislaus Malinowski looked from one to the other of the two police officers and flung back his head and laughed.

"It is very amusing!" he said. "You look solemn as owls. It is ridiculous that you should ask me to come here and wish to ask me questions. You have nothing against me, nothing."

"We think you may be able to assist us in our inquiries, Mr. Malinowski." Chief Inspector Davy spoke with official smoothness. "You own a car, Mercedes-Otto, registration number FAN 2266."

"Is there any reason why I should not own such a car?"

"No reason at all, sir. There's just a little uncertainty as to the correct number. Your car was on a highway, M. Seven, and the registration plate on that occasion was a different one."

"Nonsense. It must have been some other car."

"There aren't so many of that make. We have checked up on those there are."

"You believe everything, I suppose, that your traffic police tell you! It is laughable! Where was all this?"

"The place where the police stopped you and asked

to see your license is not very far from Bedhampton. It was on the night of the Irish Mail robbery."

"You really do amuse me," said Ladislaus Malinowski.

"You have a revolver?"

"Certainly, I have a revolver and an automatic pistol. I have proper licenses for them."

"Quite so. They are both still in your possession?"

"Certainly."

"I have already warned you, Mr. Malinowski."

"The famous policeman's warning! Anything you say will be taken down and used against you at your trial."

"That's not quite the wording," said Father mildly. "Used, yes. Against, no. You don't want to qualify that statement of yours?"

"No, I do not."

"And you are sure you don't want your solicitor here?"

"I do not like solicitors."

"Some people don't. Where are those firearms now?"

"I think you know very well where they are, Chief Inspector. The small pistol is in the pocket of my car, the Mercedes-Otto whose registered number is, as I have said, FAN 2266. The revolver is in a drawer in my flat."

"You're quite right about the one in the drawer in your flat," said Father, "but the other—the pistol—is not in your car."

"Yes, it is. It is in the left-hand pocket."

Father shook his head. "It may have been once. It isn't now. Is this it, Mr. Malinowski?"

He passed a small automatic pistol across the table. Ladislaus Malinowski, with an air of great surprise, picked it up.

"Ah-ha, yes. This is it. So it was you who took it from my car?"

"No," said Father, "we didn't take it from your car. It was not in your car. We found it somewhere else."

"Where did you find it?"

"We found it," said Father, "in an area in Pond Street which—as you no doubt know—is a street near Park Lane. It could have been dropped by a man walking down that street—or running perhaps."

Ladislaus Malinowski shrugged his shoulders. "That is nothing to do with me—I did not put it there. It was in my car a day or two ago. One does not continually look to see if a thing is still where one has put it. One assumes it will be."

"Do you know, Mr. Malinowski, that this is the pistol which was used to shoot Michael Gorman on the night of November twenty-sixth?"

"Michael Gorman? I do not know a Michael Gorman."

"The commissionaire from Bertram's Hotel."

"Ah yes, the one who was shot. I read about it. And you say my pistol shot him? Nonsense!"

"It's not nonsense. The ballistic experts have examined it. You know enough of firearms to be aware that their evidence is reliable."

"You are trying to frame me. I know what you police do!"

"I think you know the police of this country better than that, Mr. Malinowski."

"Are you suggesting that I shot Michael Gorman?"

"So far we are only asking for a statement. No charge has been made."

"But that is what you think—that I shot that ridiculous dressed-up military figure. Why should I? I didn't owe him money, I had no grudge against him."

"It was a young lady who was shot at. Gorman ran to protect her and received the second bullet in his chest."

"A young lady?"

"A young lady whom I think you know. Miss Elvira Blake."

"Do you say someone tried to shoot Elvira with my pistol?"

He sounded incredulous.

"It could be that you had had a disagreement."

"You mean that I quarrelled with Elvira and shot her? What madness! Why should I shoot the girl I am going to marry?"

"Is that part of your statement? That you are going to marry Miss Elvira Blake?"

Just for a moment or two Ladislaus hesitated. Then he said, shrugging his shoulders, "She is still very young. It remains to be discussed."

"Perhaps she had promised to marry you, and then —she changed her mind. There was someone she was afraid of. Was it you, Mr. Malinowski?"

"Why should I want her to die? Either I am in love with her and want to marry her, or if I do not want to marry her, I need not marry her. It is as simple as that. So why should I kill her?"

"There aren't many people close enough to her to want to kill her." Davy waited a moment and then said, almost casually, "There's her mother, of course."

"What!" Malinowski sprang up. "Bess? Bess kill her own daughter? You are mad! Why should Bess kill Elvira?"

"Possibly because, as next of kin, she might inherit an enormous fortune."

"Bess? You mean Bess would kill for money? She

has plenty of money from her American husband. Enough, anyway."

"Enough is not the same as a great fortune," said Father. "People do murder for a large fortune, mothers have been known to kill their children, and children have killed their mothers."

"I tell you, you're mad!"

"You say that you may be going to marry Miss Blake. Perhaps you have already married her? If so, then you would be the one to inherit a vast fortune."

"What more crazy, stupid things can you say! No, I am not married to Elvira. She is a pretty girl. I like her, and she is in love with me. Yes, I admit it. I met her in Italy. We had fun—but that is all. No more, do you understand?"

"Indeed? Just now, Mr. Malinowski, you said quite definitely that she was the girl you were going to marry."

"Oh that."

"Yes—that. Was it true?"

"I said it because—it sounded more respectable that way. You are so—prudish in this country—"

"That seems to me an unlikely explanation."

"You do not understand anything at all. The mother and I—we are lovers—I did not wish to say so—so I suggest instead that the daughter and I—we are engaged to be married. That sounds very English and proper."

"It sounds to me even more far-fetched. You're rather badly in need of money, aren't you, Mr. Malinowski?"

"My dear Chief Inspector, I am always in need of money. It is very sad."

"And yet a few months ago I understand you were flinging money about in a very carefree way."

"Ah. I had had a lucky flutter. I am a gambler. I admit it."

"I find that quite easy to believe. Where did you have this 'flutter'?"

"That I do not tell. You can hardly expect it."

"I don't expect it."

"Is that all you have to ask me?"

"For the moment, yes. You have identified the pistol as yours. That will be very helpful."

"I don't understand—I can't conceive—" he broke off and stretched out his hand. "Give it me please."

"I'm afraid we'll have to keep it for the present, so I'll write you out a receipt for it."

He did so and handed it to Malinowski.

The latter went out slamming the door.

"Temperamental chap," said Father.

"You didn't press him on the matter of the false number plate and Bedhampton?"

"No. I wanted him rattled. But not too badly rattled. We'll give him one thing to worry about at a time. And he is worried."

"The Old Man wanted to see you, sir, as soon as you were through."

Chief Inspector Davy nodded and made his way to Sir Ronald's room.

"Ah, Father. Making progress?"

"Yes. Getting along nicely—quite a lot of fish in the net. Small fry mostly. But we're closing in on the big fellows. Everything's in train—"

"Good show, Fred," said the Assistant Commissioner.

25

Miss Marple got off her train at Paddington and saw the burly figure of Chief Inspector Davy standing on the platform waiting for her.

He said, "Very good of you, Miss Marple," put his hand under her elbow and piloted her through the barrier to where a car was waiting. The driver opened the door, Miss Marple got in, Chief Inspector Davy followed her and the car drove off.

"Where are you taking me, Chief Inspector Davy?"

"To Bertram's Hotel."

"Dear me, Bertram's Hotel again. Why?"

"The official reply is: because the police think you can assist them in their inquiries."

"That sounds familiar, but surely rather sinister? So often the prelude to an arrest, is it not?"

"I am not going to arrest you, Miss Marple." Father smiled. "You have an alibi."

Miss Marple digested this in silence. Then she said, "I see."

They drove to Bertram's Hotel in silence. Miss Gorringe looked up from the desk as they entered, but Chief Inspector Davy piloted Miss Marple straight to the elevator.

"Second floor."

The elevator ascended, stopped, and Father led the way along the corridor.

As he opened the door of No. 18, Miss Marple said, "This is the same room I had when I was staying here before."

"Yes," said Father.

Miss Marple sat down in the armchair. "A very comfortable room," she observed, looking round with a slight sigh.

"They certainly know what comfort is here," Father agreed.

"You look tired, Chief Inspector," said Miss Marple unexpectedly.

"I've had to get around a bit. As a matter of fact I've just got back from Ireland."

"Indeed. From Ballygowlan?"

"Now how the devil did you know about Ballygowlan? I'm sorry—I beg your pardon."

Miss Marple smiled forgiveness.

"I suppose Michael Gorman happened to tell you he came from there—was that it?"

"No, not exactly," said Miss Marple.

"Then how, if you'll excuse me asking you, did you know?"

"Oh dear," said Miss Marple, "it's really very embarrassing. It was just something I—happened to overhear."

"Oh, I see."

"I wasn't eavesdropping. It was in a public room—at least technically a public room. Quite frankly, I enjoy listening to people talking. One does. Especially when one is old and doesn't get about very much. I mean, if people are talking near you, you listen."

"Well, that seems to me quite natural," said Father.

"Up to a point, yes," said Miss Marple. "If people do not choose to lower their voices, one must assume that they are prepared to be overheard. But of course matters may develop. The situation sometimes arises when you realize that though it is a public room, other people talking do not realize that there is anyone else in it. And then one has to decide what to do about it. Get up and cough, or just stay quite quiet and hope they won't realize you've been there. Either way is embarrassing."

Chief Inspector Davy glanced at his watch. "Look here," he said, "I want to hear more about this, but I've got Canon Pennyfather arriving at any moment. I must go and collect him. You don't mind?"

Miss Marple said she didn't mind. Chief Inspector Davy left the room.

II

Canon Pennyfather came through the swing doors into the hall of Bertram's Hotel. He frowned slightly, wondering what it was that seemed a little different about Bertram's today. Perhaps it had been painted or done up in some way? He shook his head. That was not it, but there was something. It did not occur to him that it was the difference between a six-foot commissionaire with blue eyes and dark hair and a five-foot seven commissionaire with sloping shoulders, freckles and a sandy thatch of hair bulging out under his commissionaire's cap. He just knew something was different. In his usual vague way he wandered up to the desk. Miss Gorringe was there and greeted him.

"Canon Pennyfather. How nice to see you. Have you come to fetch your baggage? It's all ready for you. If you'd only let us know, we could have sent it to you to any address you like."

"Thank you," said Canon Pennyfather, "thank you very much. You're always most kind, Miss Gorringe. But as I had to come up to London anyway today I thought I might as well call for it."

"We were so worried about you," said Miss Gorringe. "Being missing, you know. Nobody able to find you. You had a car accident, I hear?"

"Yes," said Canon Pennyfather. "Yes. People drive much too fast nowadays. Most dangerous. Not that I can remember much about it. It affected my head. Concussion, the doctor says. Oh well, as one is getting on in life, one's memory—" he shook his head sadly. "And how are you, Miss Gorringe?"

"Oh, I'm very well," said Miss Gorringe.

At that moment it struck Canon Pennyfather that Miss Gorringe also was different. He peered at her, trying to analyze where the difference lay. Her hair? That was the same as usual. Perhaps even a little frizzier. Black dress, large locket, cameo brooch. All there as usual. But there was a difference. Was she perhaps a little thinner? Or was it—yes, surely, she looked worried. It was not often that Canon Pennyfather noticed whether people looked worried, he was not the kind of man who noticed emotion in the faces of others, but it struck him today, perhaps because Miss Gorringe had so invariably presented exactly the same countenance to guests for so many years.

"You've not been ill, I hope?" he asked solicitously. "You look a little thinner."

"Well, we've had a good deal of worry, Canon Pennyfather."

"Indeed. Indeed. I'm sorry to hear it. Not due to my disappearance, I hope?"

"Oh no," said Miss Gorringe. "We worried, of course, about that, but as soon as we heard that you were all right—" She broke off and said, "No. No—it's this—well, perhaps you haven't read about it in the papers. Gorman, our doorman, got killed."

"Oh yes," said Canon Pennyfather. "I remember now. I did see it mentioned in the paper—that you had had a murder here."

Miss Gorringe shuddered at this blunt mention of the word murder. The shudder went all up her black dress.

"Terrible," she said, "terrible. Such a thing has *never* happened at Bertram's. I mean, we're not the sort of hotel where murders happen."

"No, no, indeed," said Canon Pennyfather quickly. "I'm sure you're not. I mean it would never have occurred to me that anything like that could happen here."

"Of course it wasn't inside the hotel," said Miss Gorringe, cheering up a little as this aspect of the affair struck her. "It was outside in the street."

"So really nothing to do with you at all," said the canon, helpfully.

That apparently was not quite the right thing to say.

"But it was connected with Bertram's. We had to have the police here questioning people, since it was our commissionaire who was shot."

"So that's a new man you have outside. D'you know, I thought somehow things looked a little strange."

"Yes, I don't know that he's very satisfactory. I

mean, not quite the style we're used to here. But of course we had to get someone quickly."

"I remember all about it now," said Canon Pennyfather, assembling some rather dim memories of what he had read in the paper a week ago. "But I thought it was a girl who was shot."

"You mean Lady Sedgwick's daughter? I expect you remember seeing her here with her guardian Colonel Luscombe. Apparently she was attacked by someone in the fog. I expect they wanted to snatch her bag. Anyway they fired a shot at her and then Gorman, who of course had been a soldier and was a man with a lot of presence of mind, rushed down, got in front of her and got shot himself, poor fellow."

"Very sad, very sad," said the canon, shaking his head.

"It makes everything terribly difficult," complained Miss Gorringe. "I mean, the police constantly in and out. I suppose that's to be expected, but we don't like it here, though I must say Chief Inspector Davy and Sergeant Wadell are very respectable looking. Plain clothes, and very good style, not the sort with boots and mackintoshes like one sees on films. Almost like one of us."

"Er—yes," said Canon Pennyfather.

"Did you have to go to hospital?" inquired Miss Gorringe.

"No," said the canon, "some very nice people, really Good Samaritans—a market gardener, I believe —picked me up and his wife nursed me back to health. I'm most grateful, most grateful. It is refreshing to find there is still human kindness in the world. Don't you think so?"

Miss Gorringe said she thought it was very refreshing. "After all one reads about the increase in crime," she added, "all those dreadful young men and girls holding up banks and robbing trains and ambushing people." She looked up and said, "There's Chief Inspector Davy coming down the stairs now. I think he wants to speak to you."

"I don't know why he should want to speak to me," said Canon Pennyfather, puzzled. "He's already been to see me, you know," he said, "at Chadminster. He was very disappointed, I think, that I couldn't tell him anything useful."

"You couldn't?"

The canon shook his head sorrowfully. "I couldn't remember. The accident took place somewhere near a place called Bedhampton and really I don't understand what I can have been doing there. The Chief Inspector kept asking me why I was there and I couldn't tell him. Very odd, isn't it? He seemed to think I'd been driving a car from somewhere near a railway station to vicarage."

"That sounds very possible," said Miss Gorringe.

"It doesn't seem possible at all," said Canon Pennyfather. "I mean, why should I be driving about in a part of the world that I don't really know?"

Chief Inspector Davy had come up to them. "So here you are, Canon Pennyfather," he said. "Feeling quite yourself again?"

"Oh, I feel quite well now," said the canon, "but rather inclined to have headaches still. And I've been told not to do too much. But I still don't seem to remember what I ought to remember, and the doctor says it may never come back."

"Oh well," said Chief Inspector Davy, "we mustn't give up hope." He led the canon away from the desk. "There's a little experiment I want you to try," he said. "You don't mind helping me, do you?"

When Chief Inspector Davy opened the door of Number 18, Miss Marple was still sitting in the armchair by the window.

"A good many people in the street today," she observed. "More than usual."

"Oh well—this is a way through to Berkely Square and Shepherd's Market."

"I didn't mean only passers-by. Men doing things—road repairs, a telephone repair van, a couple of private cars—"

"And what—may I ask—do you deduce from that?"

"I didn't say that I deduced anything."

Father gave her a look. Then he said, "I want you to help me."

"Of course. That is why I am here. What do you want me to do?"

"I want you to do exactly what you did on the night of November nineteenth. You were asleep—you woke up—possibly awakened by some unusual noise. You switched on the light, looked at the time, got out of bed, opened the door and looked out. Can you repeat those actions?"

"Certainly," said Miss Marple. She got up and went across to the bed.

"Just a moment."

Chief Inspector Davy went and tapped on the connecting walls of the next room.

"You'll have to do that louder," said Miss Marple. "This place is very well built."

The Chief Inspector redoubled the force of his knuckles.

"I told Canon Pennyfather to count ten," he said, looking at his watch. "Now then, off you go."

Miss Marple touched the electric lamp, looked at an imaginary clock, got up, walked to the door, opened it and looked out. To her right, just leaving his room, walking to the top of the stairs, was Canon Pennyfather. He arrived at the top of the stairs and started down them. Miss Marple gave a slight catch of her breath. She turned back.

"Well?" said Chief Inspector Davy.

"The man I saw that night can't have been Canon Pennyfather," said Miss Marple. "Not if that's Canon Pennyfather now."

"I thought you said—"

"I know. He looked like Canon Pennyfather. His hair and his clothes and everything. But he didn't walk the same way. I think—I think he must have been a younger man. I'm sorry, very sorry, to have misled you, but it wasn't Canon Pennyfather that I saw that night. I'm quite sure of it."

"You really are quite sure this time, Miss Marple."

"Yes," said Miss Marple. "I'm sorry," she added again, "to have misled you."

"You were very nearly right. Canon Pennyfather did come back to the hotel that night. Nobody saw him come in, but that wasn't remarkable. He came in after midnight. He came up the stairs, he opened the door of his room next door and he went in. What he saw or what happened next we don't know, because he can't or won't tell us. If there was only some way we could jog his memory . . ."

"There's that German word of course," said Miss Marple, thoughtfully.

"What German word?"

"Dear me, I've forgotten it now, but—"

There was a knock at the door.

"May I come in?" said Canon Pennyfather. He entered. "Was it satisfactory?"

"Most satisfactory," said Father. "I was just telling Miss Marple—you know Miss Marple?"

"Oh yes," said Canon Pennyfather, really slightly uncertain as to whether he did or not.

"I was just telling Miss Marple how we have traced your movements. You came back to the hotel that night after midnight. You came upstairs and you opened the door of your room and went in—" He paused.

Miss Marple gave an exclamation. "I remember now," she said, "what that German word is. *Doppelgänger!*"

Canon Pennyfather uttered an exclamation. "But of course," he said, "of course! How could I have forgotten? You're quite right, you know. After that film, *The Walls of Jericho,* I came back here and I came upstairs and I opened my room and I saw— extraordinary, I distinctly saw myself sitting in a chair facing me. As you say, dear lady, a *doppelgänger.* How very remarkable! And then—let me see—" He raised his eyes, trying to think.

"And then," said Father, "startled out of their lives to see you, when they thought you were safely in Lucerne, somebody hit you on the head."

26

Canon Pennyfather had been sent on his way in a taxi to the British Museum. Miss Marple had been ensconced in the lounge by the Chief Inspector. Would she mind waiting for him there for about ten minutes? Miss Marple had not minded. She welcomed the opportunity to sit and look around her and think.

Bertram's Hotel. So many memories . . . The past fused itself with the present. A French phrase came back to her: *Plus ça change, plus c'est la même chose.* She reversed the wording. *Plus c'est la même chose, plus ça change.* Both true, she thought.

She felt sad—for Bertram's Hotel and for herself. She wondered what Chief Inspector Davy wanted of her next. She sensed in him the excitement of purpose. He was a man whose plans were at last coming to fruition. It was Chief Inspector Davy's D-Day.

The life of Bertram's went on as usual. No, Miss Marple decided, *not* as usual. There was a difference, though she could not have defined where the difference lay. An underlying uneasiness, perhaps?

The doors swung open once more and this time the big bovine-looking countryman came through them and across to where Miss Marple sat.

"All set?" he inquired genially.

"Where are you taking me now?"

"We're going to pay a call on Lady Sedgwick."

"Is she staying here?"

"Yes. With her daughter."

Miss Marple rose to her feet. She cast a glance round her and murmured, "Poor Bertram's."

"What do you mean—poor Bertram's?"

"I think you know quite well what I mean."

"Well—looking at it from your point of view, perhaps I do."

"It is always sad when a work of art has to be destroyed."

"You call this place a work of art?"

"Certainly I do. So do you."

"I see what you mean," admitted Father.

"It is like when you get ground elder really badly in a border. There's nothing else you can do about it —except dig the whole thing up."

"I don't know much about gardens. But change the metaphor to dry rot and I'd agree."

They went up in the elevator and along a passage to where Lady Sedgwick and her daughter had a corner suite.

Chief Inspector Davy knocked on the door, a voice said Come in, and he entered with Miss Marple behind him.

Bess Sedgwick was sitting in a high-backed chair near the window. She had a book on her knee which she was not reading.

"So it's you again, Chief Inspector." Her eyes went past him towards Miss Marple and she looked slightly surprised.

"This is Miss Marple," explained Chief Inspector Davy. "Miss Marple—Lady Sedgwick."

"I've met you before," said Bess Sedgwick. "You were with Selina Hazy the other day, weren't you? Do sit down," she added. Then she turned towards Chief Inspector Davy again. "Have you any news of the man who shot at Elvira?"

"Not actually what you'd call news."

"I doubt if you ever will have. In a fog like that, predatory creatures come out and prowl around looking for women walking alone."

"True up to a point," said Father. "How is your daughter?"

"Oh, Elvira is quite all right again."

"You've got her here with you?"

"Yes. I rang up Colonel Luscombe—her guardian. He was delighted that I was willing to take charge." She gave a sudden laugh. "Dear old boy. He's always been urging a mother-and-daughter reunion act!"

"He may be right at that," said Father.

"Oh no, he isn't. Just at the moment, yes, I think it is the best thing." She turned her head to look out of the window and spoke in a changed voice. "I hear you've arrested a friend of mine—Ladislaus Malinowski. On what charge?"

"Not arrested," Chief Inspector Davy corrected her. "He's just assisting us with our inquiries."

"I've sent my solicitor to look after him."

"Very wise," said Father approvingly. "Anyone who's having a little difficulty with the police is very wise to have a solicitor. Otherwise they may so easily say the wrong thing."

"Even if completely innocent?"

"Possibly it's even more necessary in that case," said Father.

"You're quite a cynic, aren't you? What are you questioning him about, may I ask? Or mayn't I?"

"For one thing we'd like to know just exactly what his movements were on the night when Michael Gorman died."

Bess Sedgwick sat up sharply in her chair.

"Have you got some ridiculous idea that Ladislaus fired those shots at Elvira? They didn't even know each other."

"He could have done it. His car was just round the corner."

"Rubbish," said Lady Sedgwick robustly.

"How much did that shooting business the other night upset you, Lady Sedgwick?"

She looked faintly surprised.

"Naturally I was upset when my daughter had a narrow escape of her life. What do you expect?"

"I didn't mean that. I mean how much did the death of Michael Gorman upset you?"

"I was very sorry about it. He was a brave man."

"Is that all?"

"What more would you expect me to say?"

"You knew him, didn't you?"

"Of course. He worked here."

"You knew him a little better than that, though, didn't you?"

"What do you mean?"

"Come, Lady Sedgwick. He was your husband, wasn't he?"

She did not answer for a moment or two, though she displayed no signs of agitation or surprise.

"You know a good deal, don't you, Chief Inspector?" She sighed and sat back in her chair. "I hadn't seen him for—let me see—a great many years. Twenty—more than twenty. And then I looked out of a window one day, and suddenly recognized Micky."

"And he recognized you?"

"Quite surprising that we did recognize each other," said Bess Sedgwick. "We were only together for about a week. Then my family caught up with us, paid Micky off, and took me home in disgrace."

She sighed.

"I was very young when I ran away with him. I knew very little. Just a fool of a girl with a head full of romantic notions. He was a hero to me, mainly because of the way he rode a horse. He didn't know what fear was. And he was handsome and gay with an Irishman's tongue! I suppose really I ran away with him! I doubt if he'd have thought of it himself. But I was wild and headstrong and madly in love!" She shook her head. "It didn't last long. . . . The first twenty-four hours were enough to disillusion me. He drank and he was coarse and brutal. When my family turned up and took me back with them, I was thankful. I never wanted to see him again."

"Did your family know that you were married to him?"

"No."

"You didn't tell them?"

"I didn't think I was married."

"How did that come about?"

"We were married in Ballygowlan, but when my people turned up, Micky came to me and told me the marriage had been a fake. He and his friends had cooked it up between them, he said. By that time it seemed to me quite a natural thing for him to have done. Whether he wanted the money that was being offered him, or whether he was afraid he'd committed a breach of law by marrying me when I wasn't of age, I don't know. Anyway, I didn't doubt for a moment that what he said was true—not then."

"And later?"

She seemed lost in her thoughts. "It wasn't until—oh, quite a number of years afterwards, when I knew a little more of life, and of legal matters, that it suddenly occurred to me that probably I was married to Micky Gorman after all!"

"In actual fact, then, when you married Lord Coniston, you committed bigamy."

"And when I married Johnny Sedgwick, and again when I married my American husband, Ridgeway Becker." She looked at Chief Inspector Davy and laughed with what seemed like genuine amusement.

"So much bigamy," she said. "It really does seem very ridiculous."

"Did you ever think of getting a divorce?"

She shrugged her shoulders. "It all seemed like a silly dream. Why rake it up? I'd told Johnny, of course." Her voice softened and mellowed as she said his name.

"And what did he say?"

"He didn't care. Neither Johnny nor I were ever very law-abiding."

"Bigamy carries certain penalties, Lady Sedgwick."

She looked at him and laughed.

"Who was ever going to worry about something that had happened in Ireland years ago? The whole thing was over and done with. Micky had taken his money and gone off. Oh, don't you understand? It seemed just a silly little incident. An incident I wanted to forget. I put it aside with the things—the very many things —that don't matter in life."

"And then," said Father, in a tranquil voice, "one day in November, Michael Gorman turned up again and blackmailed you?"

"Nonsense! Who said he blackmailed me?"

Slowly Father's eyes went round to the old lady sitting quietly, very upright, in her chair.

"You." Bess Sedgwick stared at Miss Marple. "What can you know about it?"

Her voice was more curious than accusing.

"The armchairs in this hotel have very high backs," said Miss Marple. "Very comfortable they are. I was sitting in one in front of the fire in the writing room. Just resting before I went out one morning. You came in to write a letter. I suppose you didn't realize there was anyone else in the room. And so—I heard your conversation with this man Gorman."

"You listened?"

"Naturally," said Miss Marple. "Why not? It was a public room. When you threw up the window and called to the man outside, I had no idea that it was going to be a private conversation."

Bess stared at her for a moment, then she nodded her head slowly.

"Fair enough," she said. "Yes, I see. But all the same you misunderstood what you heard. Micky didn't blackmail me. He might have thought of it—but I warned him off before he could try!" Her lips curled up again in that wide generous smile that made her face so attractive. "I frightened him off."

"Yes," agreed Miss Marple. "I think you probably did. You threatened to shoot him. You handled it—if you won't think it impertinent of me to say so—very well indeed."

Bess Sedgwick's eyebrows rose in some amusement.

"But I wasn't the only person to hear you," Miss Marple went on.

"Good gracious! Was the whole hotel listening?"

"The other armchair was also occupied."

"By whom?"

Miss Marple closed her lips. She looked at Chief Inspector Davy, and it was almost a pleading glance. "If it must be done, you do it," the glance said, "but I can't . . ."

"Your daughter was in the other chair," said Chief Inspector Davy.

"Oh, no!" The cry came out sharply. "Oh, no. Not Elvira! I see—yes, I see. She must have thought—"

"She thought seriously enough of what she had overheard to go to Ireland and search for the truth. It wasn't difficult to discover."

Again Bess Sedgwick said softly: "Oh no . . ." And then: "Poor child! Even now, she's never asked me a thing. She's kept it all to herself. Bottled it up inside herself. If she'd only told me I could have explained it all to her—showed her how it didn't matter."

"She mightn't have agreed with you there," said Chief Inspector Davy. "It's a funny thing, you know," he went on, in a reminiscent, almost gossipy manner, looking like an old farmer discussing his stock and his land, "I've learned after a great many years' trial and error—I've learned to distrust a pattern when it's simple. Simple patterns are often too good to be true. The pattern of this murder the other night was like that. Girl says someone shot at her and missed. The commissionaire came running to save her, and copped it with a second bullet. That may be all true enough. That may be the way the girl saw it. But actually behind the appearances, things might be rather different.

"You said pretty vehemently just now, Lady Sedgwick, that there could be no reason for Ladislaus Malinowski to attempt your daughter's life. Well, I'll agree with you. I don't think there was. He's the sort of young man who might have a row with a woman, pull out a knife and stick it into her. But I don't think he'd hide in an area, and wait cold-bloodedly to shoot her. But supposing he wanted to shoot someone else. Screams and shots—but what has actually happened is that Michael Gorman is dead. Suppose that was actually what was meant to happen. Malinowski plans it very carefully. He chooses a foggy night, hides in the area and waits until your daughter comes up the street. He knows she's coming because he has managed to arrange it that way. He fires a shot. It's not meant to hit the girl. He's careful not to let the bullet go anywhere near her, but she thinks it's aimed at her all right. She screams. The doorman from the hotel, hearing the shot and the scream, comes rushing down the street and then Malinowski shoots the person he's come to shoot. Michael Gorman."

"I don't believe a word of it! Why on earth should Ladislaus want to shoot Micky Gorman?"

"A little matter of blackmail, perhaps," said Father.

"Do you mean that Micky was blackmailing Ladislaus? What about?"

"Perhaps," said Father, "about the things that go on at Bertram's Hotel. Michael Gorman might have found out quite a lot about that."

"Things that go on at Bertram's Hotel? What do you mean?"

"It's been a good racket," said Father. "Well planned, beautifully executed. But nothing lasts forever. Miss Marple here asked me the other day what was wrong with this place. Well, I'll answer that question now. Bertram's Hotel is to all intents and purposes the headquarters of one of the best and biggest crime syndicates that's been known for years."

27

There was silence for about a minute or a half. Then Miss Marple spoke.

"How very interesting," she said conversationally.

Bess Sedgwick turned on her. "You don't seem surprised, Miss Marple."

"I'm not. Not really. There were so many curious things that didn't seem quite to fit in. It was all too good to be true—if you know what I mean. What they call in theatrical circles, a beautiful performance. But it was a performance—not real.

"And there were a lot of little things, people claiming a friend or an acquaintance—and turning out to be wrong."

"These things happen," said Chief Inspector Davy, "but they happened too often. Is that right, Miss Marple?"

"Yes," agreed Miss Marple. "People like Selina Hazy do make that kind of mistake. But there were so many other people doing it too. One couldn't help noticing it."

"She notices a lot," said Chief Inspector Davy, speaking to Bess Sedgwick as though Miss Marple was his pet performing dog.

Bess Sedgwick turned on him sharply.

"What did you mean when you said this place was the headquarters of a crime syndicate? I should have said that Bertram's Hotel was the most respectable place in the world."

"Naturally," said Father. "It would have to be. A lot of money, time, and thought has been spent on making it just what it is. The genuine and the phony are mixed up very cleverly. You've got a superb actor manager running the show in Henry. You've got that chap, Humfries, wonderfully plausible. He hasn't got a record in this country but he's been mixed up in some rather curious hotel dealings abroad. There are some very good character actors playing various parts here. I'll admit, if you like, that I can't help feeling a good deal of admiration for the whole set-up. It has cost this country a mint of money. It's given the C.I.D. and the provincial police forces constant headaches. Every time we seemed to be getting somewhere, and put our finger on some particular incident—it turned out to be the kind of incident that had nothing to do with anything else. But we've gone on working on it, a piece there, a piece here. A garage where stacks of number plates were kept, transferable at a moment's notice to certain cars. A firm of furniture vans, a butcher's van, a grocer's van, even one or two phony postal vans. A racing driver with a racing car covering incredible distances in incredibly few minutes, and at the other end of the scale an old clergyman jogging along in his old Morris Oxford. A cottage with a market gardener in it who lends first aid if necessary and who is in touch with a useful doctor. I needn't go into it all. The ramifications seem unending. That's one half of it. The foreign visitors who come to Bertram's are the other half. Mostly from America, or from the

Dominions. Rich people above suspicion, coming here with a good lot of luxury luggage, leaving here with a good lot of luxury luggage which looks the same but isn't. Rich tourists arriving in France and not worried unduly by the Customs because the Customs don't worry tourists when they're bringing money into the country. Not the same tourists too many times. The pitcher mustn't go to the well too often. None of it's going to be easy to prove or to tie up, but it will all tie up in the end. We've made a beginning. The Cabots, for instance—"

"What about the Cabots?" asked Bess sharply.

"You remember them? Very nice Americans. Very nice indeed. They stayed here last year and they've been here again this year. They wouldn't have come a third time. Nobody ever comes here more than twice on the same racket. Yes, we arrested them when they arrived at Calais. Very well made job, that wardrobe case they had with them. It had over three hundred thousand pounds neatly stashed. Proceeds of the Bedhampton train robbery. Of course, that's only a drop in the ocean.

"Bertram's Hotel, let me tell you, is the headquarters of the whole thing! Half the staff are in on it. Some of the guests are in on it. Some of the guests are who they say they are—some are not. The real Cabots, for instance, are in Yucatan just now. Then there was the identification racket. Take Mr. Justice Ludgrove. A familiar face, bulbous nose and a wart. Quite easy to impersonate. Canon Pennyfather. A mild country clergyman, with a great white thatch of hair and a notable absent-minded behavior. His mannerisms, his way of peering over his spectacles—all very easily imitated by a good character actor."

"But what was the use of all that?" asked Bess.

"Are you really asking me? Isn't it obvious? Mr. Justice Ludgrove is seen near the scene of a bank holdup. Someone recognizes him, mentions it. We go into it. It's all a mistake. He was somewhere else at the time. But it wasn't for a while that we realized that these were all what is sometimes called 'deliberate mistakes.' Nobody's bothered about the man who had looked so like him. And doesn't look particularly like him really. He takes off his make-up and stops acting his part. The whole thing brings about confusion. At one time we had a High Court judge, an archdeacon, an admiral, a major general, all seen near the scene of a crime.

"After the Bedhampton train robbery at least four vehicles were concerned before the loot arrived in London. A racing car driven by Malinowski took part in it, a false metal box lorry, an old-fashioned Daimler with an admiral in it, and an old clergyman with a thatch of white hair in a Morris Oxford. The whole thing was a splendid operation, beautifully planned.

"And then one day the gang had a bit of bad luck. That muddle-headed old ecclesiastic, Canon Pennyfather, went off to catch his plane on the wrong day, they turned him away from the air terminal, he wandered out into Cromwell Road, went to a film, arrived back here after midnight, came up to his room of which he had the key in his pocket, opened the door, and walked in to get the shock of his life when he saw what appeared to be himself sitting in a chair facing him! The last thing the gang expected was to see the real Canon Pennyfather, supposed to be safely in Lucerne, walk in! His double was just getting ready to start off to play his part at Bedhampton when in walked the real man. They didn't know what to do but there was a quick reflex action from one member of the party. Humfries, I suspect. He hit the old man on the head, and he went down unconscious. Somebody, I think, was angry over that. Very angry. However, they examined the old boy, decided he was only knocked out, and would probably come round later and they went on with their plans. The false Canon Pennyfather left his room, went out of the hotel, and drove to the scene of activities where he was to play his part in the relay race. What they did with the real Canon Pennyfather I don't know. I can only guess. I presume he too was moved later that night, driven down in a car, taken to the market gardener's cottage which was at a spot not too far from where the train was to be held up and where a doctor could attend to him. Then, if reports came through about Canon Pennyfather having been seen in that neighbourhood, it would all fit in. It must have been an anxious moment for all concerned until he regained consciousness and they found that at least three days had been knocked out of his remembrance."

"Would they have killed him otherwise?" asked Miss Marple.

"No," said Father. "I don't think they would have killed him. Someone wouldn't have let that happen. It has seemed very clear all along that whoever ran this show had an objection to murder."

"It sounds fantastic," said Bess Sedgwick. "Utterly fantastic! And I don't believe you have any evidence whatever to link Ladislaus Malinowski with this rigmarole."

"I've plenty of evidence against Ladislaus Malinowski," said Father. "He's careless, you know. He hung around here when he shouldn't have. On the first occasion he came to establish connnection with your daughter. They had a code arranged."

"Nonsense. She told you herself that she didn't know him."

"She may have told me that but it wasn't true. She's in love with him. She wants the fellow to marry her."

"I don't believe it!"

"You're not in a position to know," Chief Inspector Davy pointed out. "Malinowski isn't the sort of person who tells all his secrets and your daughter you don't know at all. You admitted as much. You were angry, weren't you, when you found out Malinowski had come to Bertram's Hotel."

"Why should I be angry?"

"Because you're the brains of the show," said Father. "You and Henry. The financial side was run by the Hoffman brothers. They made all the arrangements with the Continental banks and accounts and that sort of thing, but the boss of the syndicate, the brains that run it, and plan it, are your brains, Lady Sedgwick."

Bess looked at him and laughed. "I never heard anything so ridiculous!" she said.

"Oh no, it's not ridiculous at all. You've got brains, courage and daring. You've tried most things; you thought you'd turn your hand to crime. Plenty of excitement in it, plenty of risk. It wasn't the money that attracted you, I'd say, it was the fun of the whole thing. But you wouldn't stand for murder, or for undue violence. There were no killings, no brutal assaults, only nice quiet scientific taps on the head if necessary. You're a very interesting woman, you know. One of the few really interesting great criminals."

There was silence for some few minutes. Then Bess Sedgwick rose to her feet.

"I think you must be mad." She put her hand out to the telephone.

"Going to ring up your solicitor? Quite the right thing to do before you say too much."

With a sharp gesture she slammed the receiver back on the hook.

"On second thoughts I hate solicitors. . . . All right. Have it your own way. Yes, I ran this show. You're quite correct when you say it was fun. I loved every minute of it. It was fun scooping money from banks, trains and post offices and so-called security vans! It was fun planning and deciding; glorious fun and I'm glad I had it. The pitcher goes to the well once too often? That's what you said just now, wasn't it? I suppose it's true. Well, I've had a good run for my money! But you're wrong about Ladislaus Malinowski shooting Michael Gorman! He didn't. I did." She laughed a sudden high, excited laugh.

"Never mind what it was he did, what he threatened . . . I told him I'd shoot him—Miss Marple heard me —and I did shoot him. I did very much what you suggested Ladislaus did. I hid in that area. When Elvira passed, I fired one shot wild, and when she screamed and Micky came running down the street, I'd got him where I wanted him, and I let him have it! I've got keys to all the hotel entrances, of course. I just slipped in through the area door and up to my room. It never occurred to me you'd trace the pistol to Ladislaus— or would even suspect him. I'd pinched it from his car without his knowing. But not, I can assure you, with any idea of thowing suspicion on him."

She swept round on Miss Marple. "You're a witness to what I've said, remember. I killed Gorman."

"Or perhaps you are saying so because you're in love with Malinowski," suggested Davy.

"I'm not." Her retort came sharply. "I'm his good friend, that's all. Oh yes, we've been lovers in a casual kind of way, but I'm not in love with him. In all my life, I've only loved one person—John Sedgwick." Her voice changed and softened as she pronounced the name.

"But Ladislaus is my friend. I don't want him railroaded for something he didn't do. I killed Michael Gorman. I've said so, and Miss Marple has heard me. . . . And now, dear Chief Inspector Davy—" Her voice rose excitedly, and her laughter rang out: "Catch me if you can."

With a sweep of her arm, she smashed the window with the heavy telephone set, and before Father could get to his feet, she was out of the window and edging her way rapidly along the narrow parapet. With surprising quickness in spite of his bulk, Davy had moved to the other window and flung up the sash. At the same time he blew the whistle he had taken from his pocket.

Miss Marple, getting to her feet with rather more difficulty a moment or two later, joined him. Together they stared out along the façade of Bertram's Hotel.

"She'll fall. She's climbing up a drainpipe," Miss Marple exclaimed. "But why *up?*"

"Going to the roof. It's her only chance and she knows it. Good God, look at her. Climbs like a cat. She looks like a fly on the side of the wall. The risks she's taking!"

Miss Marple murmured, her eyes half closing, "She'll fall. She can't do it. . . ."

The woman they were watching disappeared from sight. Father drew back a little into the room.

Miss Marple asked, "Don't you want to go and—"

Father shook his head. "What good am I with my bulk? I've got my men posted ready for something like this. They know what to do. In a few minutes we shall know. . . . I wouldn't put it past her to beat the lot of them! She's a woman in a thousand, you know." He sighed. "One of the wild ones. Oh, we've some of them in every generation. You can't tame them, you can't bring them into the community and make them live in law and order. They go their own way. If they're saints, they go and tend lepers or something, or get themselves martyred in jungles. If they're bad lots, they commit the atrocities that you don't like hearing about. And sometimes—they're just wild! They'd have been all right, I suppose, born in another age when it was everyone's hand for himself, everyone fighting to keep life in their viens. Hazards at every turn, danger all round them, and they themselves perforce dangerous to others. That world would have suited them; they'd have been at home in it. This one doesn't."

"Did you know what she was going to do?"

"Not really. That's one of her gifts. The unexpected. She must have thought this out, you know. She knew what was coming. So she sat looking at us—keeping the ball rolling—and thinking. Thinking and planning hard. I expect—ah—" He broke off as there came the sudden roar of a car's exhaust, the screaming of wheels, and the sound of a big racing engine. He leaned out. "She's made it, she's got to her car."

There was more screaming as the car came round the corner on two wheels, a great roar, and the beautiful white monster came tearing up the street.

"She'll kill someone," said Father, "she'll kill a lot of people . . . even if she doesn't kill herself."

"I wonder," said Miss Marple.

"She's a good driver, of course. A damned good driver. Whoof, that was a near one!"

They heard the roar of the car racing away with

the horn blaring, heard it grow fainter. Heard cries, shouts, the sound of brakes, carshooting and pulling up and finally a great scream of tires and a roaring exhaust and—

"She's crashed," said Father.

He stood there very quietly waiting with the patience that was characteristic of his whole big patient form. Miss Marple stood silent beside him. Then, like a relay race, word came down along the street. A man on the pavement opposite, looked up at Chief Inspector Davy and made rapid signs with his hands.

"She's had it," said Father heavily. "Dead! Went about ninety miles an hour into the park railings. No other casualties bar a few slight collisions. Magnificent driving. Yes, she's dead." He turned back into the room and said heavily, "Well, she told her story first. You heard her."

"Yes," said Miss Marple. "I heard her." There was a pause. "It wasn't true, of course," said Miss Marple quietly.

Father looked at her. "You didn't believe her, eh?"

"Did you?"

"No," said Father. "No, it wasn't the right story. She thought it out so that it would meet the case exactly, but it wasn't true. She didn't shoot Michael Gorman. D'you happen to know who did?"

"Of course I know," said Miss Marple. "The girl."

"Ah! When did you begin to think that?"

"I always wondered," said Miss Marple.

"So did I," said Father. "She was full of fear that night. And the lies she told were poor lies. But I couldn't see a motive at first."

"That puzzled me," said Miss Marple. "She had found out her mother's marriage was bigamous, but would a girl do murder for that? Not nowadays! I suppose—there was a money side to it?"

"Yes, it was money," said Chief Inspector Davy. "Her father left her a colossal fortune. When she found out that her mother was married to Michael Gorman, she realized that the marriage to Coniston hadn't been legal. She thought that meant that the money wouldn't come to her because, though she was his daughter, she wasn't legitimate. She was wrong, you know. We had a case something like that before. Depends on the terms of a will. Coniston left it quite clearly to her, naming her by name. She'd get it all right, but she didn't know that. And she wasn't going to let go of the cash."

"Why did she need it so badly?"

Chief Inspector Davy said grimly, "To buy Ladislaus Malinowski. He would have married her for her money. He wouldn't have married her without it. She wasn't a fool, that girl. She knew that. But she wanted him on any terms. She was desperately in love with him."

"I know," said Miss Marple. She explained, "I saw her face that day in Battersea Park. . . ."

"She knew that with the money she'd get him, and without the money she'd lose him," said Father. "And so she planned a cold-blooded murder. She didn't hide in the area, of course. There was nobody in the area. She just stood by the railings and fired a shot and screamed, and when Michael Gorman came racing down the street from the hotel, she shot him at close quarters. Then she went on screaming. She was a cool hand. She'd no idea of incriminating young Ladislaus. She pinched his pistol because it was the only way she could get hold of one easily; and she never dreamed that he would be suspected of the crime, or that he